AMITYVILLE
DEATH TOILET

THE NOVELIZATION

BRIAN G. BERRY

BASED ON THE ORIGINAL SCREENPLAY BY
EVAN JACOBS

Encyclopocalypse Publications
www.encyclopocalypse.com

FOREWORD
BY EVAN JACOBS

AMITYVILLE DEATH TOILET started off, like a lot of SRS projects, with Ron Bonk (SRS CINEMA owner) texting me.

How much are you making DEATH TOILETS for these days? He asked.

However much you need me to make them for, I replied.

Ron proceeded to tell me that he had a movie he wanted me to make. That I had to keep it a secret. I figured he'd tell me in a few days or a week or whatever.

AMITYVILLE DEATH TOILET he wrote back immediately.

There were a few stipulations. Whatever happened in the movie, it needed a standalone plot and I couldn't use footage from the other DEATH TOILET films, but I could use the same characters, and reference the other movies.

That wasn't going to be a problem. After shooting, directing, and editing the first four DEATH TOILET movies, I was more than happy to not jump back into a film with Father Dingleberry and Brett Baxter. Not that I have anything against those characters, but I just needed a break from the formula of these two somehow convincing the other that there were still more toilets to exorcize, and then throwing explosions all over the place to help them do it. And making it a completely unrelated story would make it easier. Other than being a "DEATH TOILET" movie, it wouldn't need to artificially tie itself to that series of films.

Also, porting DEATH TOILET into the realm of Amityville would be funny. On top of that, I knew I was going to use the DEATH TOILET guys Mike Hartsfield (Bax) and Isaac (Father D) in AMITYVILLE DEATH TOILET.

My idea was that this film would explore ghost hunter shows and social media, and hopefully make a statement about it all within the rich milieu of the Amityville/DEATH TOILET worlds.

The success, interest, or sheer curiosity surrounding AMITYVILLE DEATH TOILET truly makes me smile. It has done much more than I ever thought it would. From appearing on YouTube shows where they pick apart how awful they think the film is, to reviews saying that AMITYVILLE DEATH TOILET is actually a good film, to mentions in articles about much bigger movies like NIGHT SWIM, this 70 minute opus just keeps going. I guess this book is the next chapter in the life of this irrepressible film.

I can only take some of the credit, though.

Those opening scenes in which Mike Hartsfield, playing three different characters who gets killed in three different ways by the toilet, only exist because of how Mike played them and set up the FX. Sure, I had some ideas but he's always been excellent at bringing them to life. The only thing I take credit for is the toilet cleaner, somehow being commanded by the Death Toilet, to choke Mike's ill dressed character to death. I just added the sound fx and slowed down the video. The rest is all Mike.

Which brings us to Isaac Golub's portrayal of Gregg

G. Allin. From the name of the main character he embodied (evoking the late, feces coated, punk singer no less), to the hairstyle and clothes, to the endless ad-libbing, and physical comedy, Isaac was a rare talent. He was probably best known for fronting the hardcore/punk, straight-edge band A CHORUS OF DISAPPROVAL, but I always thought that he could be great at anything he put his mind to. Whether it was creating props, wardrobes, music, making food, doing his musical departure called COUNT CATASTROPHIC, Isaac did it well and if he did it for you then you wanted him to keep doing it. This is why I kept putting him in my movies. I just enjoyed seeing him do whatever he was doing on screen. Sadly, he was killed in an auto accident on April 28th, 2023.

I'd like to dedicate this book to Isaac and his family.

At the start of this forward, I talked about needing a break from exercising toilets and never-ending explosions. Well, if you've seen AMITYVILLE DEATH TOILET you're probably aware that it doesn't deviate too much from the plot of the other four death toilet films that came before it. Gregg G. Allin tries to figure out how a toilet could be killing people, and then he conquers it via copious amounts of bad, computer generated explosions.

If any movie ever needed to be made, or needed a novelization, it most certainly is AMITYVILLE DEATH TOILET. Thank you to Ron Bonk and Brian G. Berry for making it all happen!

Evan Jacobs
Anhedenia Films Unlimited

In memory of and dedicated to
Isaac Golub

PRESENTS

AMITYVILLE
DEATH TOILET

ONE

John was having a great morning. Yes sir, he was out of bed, feeling the warmth of the sun coming through the windows. He even opened those windows, basking in the cool breeze sweeping up the street, stirring bushes and trees. It brought the smell of late spring to him. A clean smell, a budding aroma that made you feel good to be alive. John had a wonderful day planned ahead too. Since he was off work for the next two days, he decided what he needed most was to just lounge around the house and not do a goddamn thing. Not a finger to be lifted unless it was to make himself a snack or punch the numbers on the phone for a pizza.

Lazing about on the couch, John winced at a sharp pain cutting through his abdomen. It started low in his groin, then swung high, boiling in his gut, spreading hip to hip. "Oh God, what the hell . . ."

Hoping to dissuade the pain, he rubbed at his belly, picked the remote up, and clicked through the channels. Since nothing worthy of attention was catching his eye, he left it on the station where a big brown dog and his shaggy-looking friend were bolting up a cobwebbed hallway away from a bulky monster with its mouth dropped open, jammed full of teeth. He cracked a smile when the dog tripped on its paws and went sliding forward, bringing his idiotic companion with him.

"Oh shit . . ." There it was again, that stabbing pain in his belly. It felt just like a knife would feel, he figured. Like someone teasing the tip along the skin, giving it some taps. "Ow!" This time, the sensation of a blade retreated with the onset of something worse. Felt like he took a shot of molten iron. "Goddamn. Fuck." As he rubbed his lower belly, the pain ebbed down in and around his thighs, and out of his butthole squealed a whistle that turned to a flapping, flatulent rattle that drew his eyes closed with pain. "Oh God. Oh God."

As he gently put his feet on the ground, John, leaning over and holding his gut, made himself walk out of the living room and into the guest bathroom. The whole way, his knees buckling, he popped enough gas to enforce a biological lockdown of the town. He was lucky to make the toilet in time and double thankful for the grace his gut gave him by allowing him to drag his pants to the ground.

Settling in for the evacuation, still bent, he let it go. Instantly, the toilet bowl was awash, under attack by a butthole blowing its load like a pressurized tap gone apeshit. So absolutely vile was the smell wafting up below him, his face responded in kind by scrunching. "God, what did I eat?"

That was the question cycling in his mind while his anal cavity widened out as chunks upon chunks of feculent links gushed out on a rapid of foaming fecal fluids.

He was stinking up the place bad, stomping his feet as it seemed this hell would never abate. But another minute cruised by when a reprieve was gifted and John smiled weakly, followed by a long sigh from the exertion. "Finally . . . Finally it's over." He went to reach for the toilet paper when it started to spin wickedly fast and threw a ribbon of it in the air. Startled, John let his hand fall and leaned away as it continued to spin and spin and throw out a long ribbon. "Agh! What the hell?"

The first square of the ribbon sprung at him, coiling his wrist and circling higher up his arm.

"HELP!"

He tried to stem the toilet paper as it wound up and up, finding his neck and giving it a light strangle.

"No! HELP!"

From the basket of extra rolls behind him on the tank lid, more toilet paper spun out of control, flinging multiple ribbons upward, several of which swung out and took his right hand at the wrist and pinned him down. Now his ankles, too, were under siege, coiling with 2-ply circling up his legs, past his knees.

Shaken up and whining, John released another payload, which blew from between his buttocks like a blast of buckshot. "HELP! SOMEONE HELP ME!" Strands of toilet paper were tightening around his throat, traveling up around his face until just his eyes were left, popped open wide, strained and frightened.

His screams were muffled now, and his hands and feet were useless. He was effectively shut down. A prisoner shackled by hundreds of feet of toilet paper.

Such a huge waste, he thought, despite the absurdity of thinking such a thing. He fought against his binds, but there was no leverage. It seemed the more he fought, the tighter the paper constricted.

There was no escape.

Not for John.

His eyes darted left and right when he felt something tickling his butthole. He couldn't be sure, but it felt like a finger exploring his sphincter. A single finger, as if someone's hand was down there in the toilet water attempting to test his prostate. He tried to kick and he

3

mumbled a scream when the finger became a fist and punched right up into his rectum, coring to the large intestine. He tried to dislodge the intruder by swinging his hips and rocking to no avail. The fist, or whatever it was, was aggressively exploring his insides. His eyes rolled over to the white of boiled eggs when the feeling of digits curled around his liver and gave it a tug. His body jerked with convulsions, spreading with violent tremors as the organ was yanked down until it popped from his anus.

But that wasn't the end of it.

Everything packed inside of him exploded from his ass until the toilet bowl was overflowing with shit and blood and meat. His body slowly deflated as even his bones shattered, sliding right out of the ruined aperture of his anal cavity. It was like a vacuum had plugged itself into his body and sucked it all clean. Left with only minor bones and muscle, his skin sagged, collapsing like a rubber suit. The only thing remaining was his skull. And to finish that off, a butcher knife appeared from behind the toilet, wielded by a smoky arm. It took one swipe to John's head and split the thing to the chin. His brain tumbled out, splatting against the shitty, bloody pool spreading out from the base of the toilet.

And when it was over, a mighty flush took everything inside that bowl and sucked it down into the pipes.

The only things marking his death were a few fragments of skull and his brain, resting in a pool of shit-blood.

Two

Connor, over the moon about his birthday, was hopping and dancing around in the bathroom, styling his thick dark hair while swinging his hips to a song in his head. He brought the brush to his mouth and started singing, winking at the mirror and busting back into his dance routine.

After all, what kid wasn't excited about getting their driver's license for the first time? Connor had been waiting all year for this day. He was ready. His parents had been teaching him to drive for six months, and he took to it naturally.

Now he just needed a car of his own so he wouldn't have to beg and borrow his parent's vehicle—which would be so uncool considering they drove a hunter green minivan. He was hoping that's why his dad left the house early today, to go pick up a car for his birthday. It wasn't so far-fetched to believe. His father had recently received a big bonus from the plant and kept bragging to them how big it was this year. Connor didn't care if the car was a bucket, as long as it got him and his friends to the mall and other places they wished to go.

Brushing through his hair, Connor leaned against

the counter to get a better look at his face. "Oh no. No . . . not today!"

Yep. A zit. A big fucking zit too. Like the size of a pea, right there on the end of his nose. "How am I supposed to get rid of this?!" He tried to squeeze it but stopped, worrying that if it didn't pop, he would only make it worse. He'd been through that game before. One time, he tried to do away with one on his chin and pinched the thing until he was red in the face. But no matter how much pinching and straining, the pimple wouldn't budge. In fact, it had grown to twice its girth and was red as a blood blister.

Looking at the one planted on his nose now, he had a flashback to that day. "Great, I'm supposed to meet up with Jennifer later today. Just great!"

"Something wrong?" his mother called from outside the bathroom door.

"No, Mom, just dealing with a pimple crisis."

"Uh-oh. I don't think we have any more cream either."

Oh good, Mom, what would cream do for it at a time like this? That's to prevent, not destroy! "Thanks, Mom."

Sighing, he kept staring at it in the mirror. "Hmm . . . maybe Mom has something in her bathroom I can clean this up with."

Setting the brush on the counter, he grabbed the knob to the door.

Locked.

He tried it again, thinking he twisted it wrong. "Hey, what's going on?"

He shook the thing, placing his hand against the door. "Come on, open! How can it be locked?"

The toilet flushing brought him around.

"What . . ." The lid was up and black smoke was rising out of the bowl. "What's going on?" He took a step forward, straining his neck to see into the bowl. "That's so weird. Mom!"

As the word left his mouth, his eyes widened at the frame of a gun suddenly shimmering to life, hooked to the flushing handle. It was a big cannon of a pistol, black as the smoke coming out of the toilet bowl. "Wait — No . . . wait!" Its barrel was pointed right at him. "No! This can't be happening!"

BAM! Connor was thrown back to the wall, a hole as big as a cantaloupe in his chest. *BAM!* The shot tore his back open and sprayed blood up the wall. *BAM!* A devastating hit that punched his head flat peppered the wall and ceiling with blood and brain.

His body slid to the ground, leaving a thick scarlet smear behind him.

"Connor, what was that noise?" asked his mom as she opened the door and saw her sixteen-year-old son's bloody body on the floor.

Her scream shook the birds from the trees.

THREE

"Hey, man, do you mind if I use your bathroom really quick?"

Clay set his beer down on the coffee table and hooked a thumb over his right shoulder. "Not at all, dude. Down the hall to the left."

Mark locked the door behind him.

Stepping up to the toilet, he swung the lid back, pulled his penis out, and gave it a few yanks. As he released himself, he spent his time roving the walls around him. From the flower pattern wallpaper, the overpowering scent of potpourri, the pink bath rugs and toilet lid cover, and the shower curtain—also pink, spotted with rose petals—he knew this was Dianne's choice of decor. He smiled thinking about Clay coming in here in his dirty work boots every day, plopping down on the toilet, and emptying the day's lunch in there.

"Clay, ol' buddy," he said to himself, smiling. "At least Dianne's got a nice set of tits on her. It's too bad her interior decorating skills are a bit shitty."

As Mark was shaking out the last few drops, the toilet water exploded in an upward surge. The power of it took him off his feet and slammed him back hard. He grunted as he slipped, smacking his face on the toilet rim, blood and teeth bursting from his mouth. He went to say something but couldn't articulate words properly and all that came out was a dismantled set of vowels dripping with beads of blood. The blow to his mouth had exacted a toll beyond cracking a few teeth; it severed his tongue midway. Leveraging his hands on the toilet bowl, he pushed to stand and made it a foot up when a knife appeared from deep in the bowl like an apparition. At first a powdery swirl, the knife hardened out with a silver blade as shiny as polished steel and edged to a razor. Mark's eyes drew open so wide you'd think they'd been replaced with golf balls. He couldn't be certain he was seeing this. He had to blink several times.

I'm knocked out, that's it. I'm dreaming!

But feeling the blood run hot from his mouth, reality tugged at his balls and dropped him front and center of what he was facing. How could you put this into perspective to believe? It contradicted everything he'd known to be real, raped his mind of the logical, and stuffed it full of the fantastical. The knife had an arm, only he couldn't make it out as everything in front of him had become a blurry diversion of funny colors and miasmic vapors. It flicked out and cut the lips from his mouth, swinging a second time and shaving his nose from his face. A third swipe took the skin off his forehead and sent it splatting to the door where it slapped against the wood like a slice of deli meat. More slabs were taken in like manner as Mark was bound by some immovable element, at the mercy of this swinging, ghostly knife. It worked his skin free until a bloody skull was left, bleeding out and pebbling Dianne's pink rug. The knife slipped away as the entire toilet started to fracture, running with intersecting hairline cracks and pieces of it falling to the floor.

Mark was shaking so bad he figured he'd shake his heart right out of his throat. All the man could do was kneel there like some acolyte, offering his life to this porcelain god. But what was coming to term beneath its glassy shell was anything but a god—it was a *demon*. Something black from Hell. Or some such place equally as nefarious. Shaped into a toilet, Mark's fingers were feeling not ceramic, but skin—hot, pebbly skin. And he wasn't looking at the toilet tank anymore, but a mouth as big as his torso, and it was opening up like the focus lens on a camera, showing Mark all of those big bad teeth inside, huge and tusklike. They were excreting some sort of bilious runoff.

Mark screamed. It came out with the timbre of a female in distress just as that big mouth hurled its lips over his body and sucked him into its maw, crunching down until his bones cracked and blood burst and sprayed, crashing onto the walls like water. The monster toilet chewed him down to the ankles and slurped those things up like a couple of noodles.

Clay was at the door, knocking. "Mark, are you okay in there? I heard some screaming and banging. Let me in."

The door opened on its own and swung back in a slow arc, giving Clay just enough room to see his wife's bathroom no longer pink and bright with girly colors, but dripping crimson, the walls flecked with meat, and the toilet shattered to a mound, the pipe bubbling with blood.

FOUR

Mayor Dump was in a mood. Not like he was ever happy about anything, but ever since the murders reported in town—toilet murders of all things—he was two steps from needing a heart transplant and his mind flinging over the edge.

Toilet murders. That's about the stupidest thing I've ever heard! It's preposterous! This can't be real!

But it was. And the police reports testified to that. Only problem was, there was no suspect, just a goddamn toilet. And how the hell were you supposed to read a toilet its rights and slap the cuffs on it? The other problem he was facing was that this wasn't localized to one toilet; it involved *multiple* toilets.

The papers had a field day. "The Amityville Toilet Massacre" and "Bloodbath in Amityville, Toilet Murderer Still on the Loose!"

They thought that shit was funny.

But not Mayor Dump.

Now, since those murders, the only toilet causing pain to the city was one such toilet in one such house. The Amityville House, as people were calling it, among other names. Killed the last several families who bought the place.

For Mayor Dump, it was the Pain-in-the-ass House. Because that's what it was giving him. Here he was, trying to encourage tourism to the city, and what he ran into instead was a whole load of interference—namely, toilet massacre fever. People were running scared, and there wasn't a lot he could do about it. He tried to have the house wiped off the map. But the companies he employed for the job turned their backs on him, saying they were frightened.

After Dump laughed his ass off, and shoved a few four-letter words down their throats while inquiring about the lack of testicles between their legs, he pressed them for answers. And boy, the ones they laid on him were just absolutely hysterical. He could have laughed his skin off. In fact, he laughed so hard that day he about dropped to the floor and rolled around. It was *that* goddamn funny to him.

To think, grown men, afraid of ghosts. Saying to him with a straight face that there were funny things in there, whispers in the air, scratching on the walls.

That was unbelievable to Mayor Dump. It was kid shit. "Will you idiots stop acting like a bunch of fucking toddlers crying for mommy and take care of this house?!"

But they walked, and Mayor Dump, so full of the piss and vinegar he once felt in his youth, marched inside that house and puffed his chest out. "Listen here, you ghoulie bastards, I'm not fucking around. You get out of my town or I'll burn this fucking house to the ground! You under—"

And it was right before he could finish his threat that a force of wind from inside the house had taken him like a giant fist and hurled him through the door. He landed fifteen feet outside, nearly breaking his neck. When he turned his face to look up at the house, he saw something that changed him. It wasn't a house anymore, not of wood and windows, but a *face*. An evil, monstrous aspect pushing through the front of the home like a hologram projection.

Of course, he never admitted it. He pushed it out of his mind, bottled it up tight, and buried it. There was no need to tell anyone. Who would believe him anyway?

As it stood, things had been getting crazy. Two squatters bedded down in the Amityville House just the other night and were discovered the next morning by the police—or pieces of them, at least. According to the officers, there wasn't much left but a few scraps and some scattered bones. This stamped the front page and now people were losing their shit—not literally, of course. They feared using their own toilets and threatened to take to the streets, demanding justice and that the town vanquish the house once and for all.

It was a never-ending cycle of bullshit, and it was starting to smell really bad.

"Chief, Chief, listen to me now, damn it," Mayor Dump said, his dress shirt worked open at the top from stressing hands, his gray hair a ruin of strands. This is Amityville, you remember? The tourists will start flocking in soon, and since those reports of the squatters, people are getting scared. The toilet, Chief, your men said it must have been the toilet again. You know how bad this looks on me? What am I going to do about the tourists, huh? These local idiots are taking to the streets! I need this stopped! We have three goddamn weeks until the season kicks off, and I want you on these streets. I want every deputy and recruit and anyone that even looks like a cop helping disband these marches!"

"What about the toilet?" the chief asked, unamused by this pompous bastard in office. They were always the same when you got them in power. At first, they were kind, holding babies and smiling, throwing out promises that turned into lies. Then, when they take office, it's about career and money. Fucking pricks.

"What do you mean? Take care of it! It's your job to do this. Or have you forgotten?"

"We're doing our best, Mayor. But what the hell can I do about a toilet? Shoot it? Rip it out of the ground? Maybe you don't remember the great Toilet Raid last year. Do I need to remind you?"

The Toilet Raid. Or as the papers painted it, "Amityville Police or SS Death Squads?"

Cops went on a rampage, storming houses around town and ripping toilets out, many with people still on them. And besides taking sledges to the porcelain thrones, officers opened up with automatic weapons, busting them into smoking chips. The police estimated they killed over three hundred toilets and lost a handful of citizens who didn't know the meaning of "Stay the fuck out of our way."

The townsfolk were livid with the chief and his men, and there was still an ongoing court order and investigation looking into the "Brutal and Militant Invasions of Taxpayers' Homes."

But the real asshole behind the trigger was Mayor Dump himself. He ordered the attack and signed on the line ratifying the Toilet Raid. And before his ink could dry, he tossed the papers into the burn file.

Yeah, you could say the chief and Dump were butting heads. And with the addition of two more murders—toilet murders—in town, things were looking bad.

"No reminder needed, Chief. But what I want is your cooperation. You take care of this before it spreads. I want plumbers, toilet technicians, pipe specialists, fecal examiners—I want anyone who has experience handling toilet affairs on this goddamn case! We have three weeks, Chief! Three weeks to end this!"

Chief Taylor Balls slammed the phone down and sighed, rubbing his temples. "God, I hate that man."

"Mayor Dump again, Chief?"

Balls raised his head. Deputy Jake Urinal was standing there, beaming as always. "Who else causes me to rub my temples in this manner?"

"What's up his ass this time?"

"Besides a prostate the size of a bowling ball, he's freaking out about the tourists again. And the toilet."

"What's our next move?"

Chief Balls sat back in his chair and plucked a cigarette from his breast pocket. "I think we've done as much as we can do as police officers. Our guns can only do so much." Urinal's face fell down a level, reliving a trauma implanted in him since the Toilet Raid. "So I have to use alternate methods."

"Which means?"

Balls shook his head as he lit up a Winston. "Paranormal shit."

FIVE

Greg G Allin, The Ghost Hunter.

That's what they call him since, on his show, that's the moniker he goes by. You see, GG Allin is an important figurehead in the paranormal biz. You want to find where that ghost is hiding in your home or sniff his butthole, GG Allin is the man you want handling business. One call to him and your poltergeist is a memory. No more freaky "boos" in the night or funny shadows spilling up the walls or slipping off the premises once the lights come on. His YouTube channel is huge, and most of his subscribers refer to him as the "Ghostbuster" or some other such lingo picked up in a movie. Only, those were classic films, with great plots and funny casting. He was the real deal, GG Allin. He might not have had the fancy ghost-fighting plasma sprayer, but he had a way about his intellect, a drive to him that could chase away the worst ghosts any spooky graveyard, abandoned asylum, or haunted house could throw at him.

Down to a few days left of his vacation, Greg was lounging in a chair at The Continental's poolside, his bare chest baking in the sun, black shades covering his eyes. It amazed him that it was his show—his channel

—that brought in the dough for him to take such a vacation. He was grateful for it and would continue to entertain folks for as long as ghosts found it necessary to scurry the hallways and attics and basements of people's homes.

Beep. Beep.

He reached for his phone, slid his thumb over the green dot, and said, "GG Allin here. Oh hey, yeah, I'm just hanging poolside. Just finished a heavy lunch and I figured I'd lay out in the sun and maybe sweat off some of those calories." He tipped his head forward and, with a pair of hungry eyes, followed after the stunning beauty in her mocha brown bikini, her skin the proper hue of coppertone, her breasts packed against the material of her top like two footballs begging for a touchdown. "Oh yeah. No, I'm not sure when I'll return. The show is doing great! I get new subscribers every day." A vibration on his cheek and he brought his phone away from his face. "There it is, I got another three subs just now. You see, it's going awesome. If it wasn't for them, I wouldn't be out here today. I might just extend my trip another week if the cash keeps stacking into the account like this." He hadn't taken his eyes off the goddess and got a perfect view of her backside as she leaned over for a dive. She splashed and came up, swinging her dark hair over her back. "Oh— Hold on a minute, I'm getting another call." He checked the phone screen and bunched his brows at the number. It wasn't familiar, so that meant it had to be a job. Maybe it would cover the funds spent on this vacation. He thumb-swiped the green dot. "Hello, this is GG Allin. Yes,"—he laughed— "The Ghost Man. You what?" He leaned forward, sitting all the way up, lowering his sunglasses. "Let me see if I got you straight: there's been a rash of killings in Amityville . . . by *toilets?* Is that what you just told me?" He had to excuse himself with a laugh. And not any

17

typical ha ha, but a drawn-out guffaw that turned some heads, including the woman in the pool. He came back on the line. "Toilets . . . killing people? Is this some sort of joke? I've had plenty of people feed me loads of ridiculousness, so if this is a joke, I'm done laughing."

Chief Balls could already say he didn't think much of this character. He had this self-assured way about him that was getting under his skin. He wished he could reach through the phone and take that apple in his neck and pluck it out of there, maybe take a bite or two, then slap it back in. "Listen, Ghost Man. I ain't pulling your grapes. We have an honest-to-God killer toilet here. And we've come to believe this ain't someone wearing a costume."

"So, you're telling me it's . . . *haunted*? Inhabited?"

"If that's the way you want to call it, then we'll go with that. That toilet is powered by spirits as far as everyone around here is concerned. And the police department of Amityville ain't equipped to handle spirit apprehension."

"How did you find me?"

"It wasn't hard. I simply put *Ghost Hunter* in Google and you were the first face to pop up. I browsed your channel and saw that you've dealt with shit like this before. Just tell me . . . you ain't one of those fake ones, are you? Because if I fly you out here on taxpayer money, we're gonna have a problem."

"No, I'm not a fake one. I'm the real McCoy. If you have a haunting, I'll pull the plug. The only thing I require is full access and the fulfillment of any requests I may have."

"Look, I ain't fixing to buy you lunch or anything like—"

"That's not what I meant. I meant any equipment or personnel I might need to assist me in capturing this . . . entity of yours."

"If that's all, I'll ring Mayor Dump and send him word that you're on the case."

"Okay, so, let me get this straight . . ."

"Go on."

Greg had to ask because he wasn't sure if he heard that right. "You're Chief Balls of the Amityville Police Department, and your mayor is . . . Dump? *Mayor Dump?*"

"That's right. Why are you laughing? What's so damn funny?"

"Nothing, nothing at all. Excuse me. I'll take the case. I'll pack now and head to the airport. I can be there in the next three hours."

"Fair enough. I'll send the details to your phone in the next thirty minutes. And when you get here, you'll be picked up by Deputy Jake Urinal."

Greg pulled a face that might have gotten him a good slap if Chief Balls were to see it. "Uh, okay, Deputy *Urinal*. I won't forget that name."

"Be sure you don't, Ghost Man. Now if you'll excuse me, I have work to do."

Greg made sure the call had ended before he started laughing.

SIX

It wasn't so bad a flight. He stayed chill most of the two hours it took to reach Amityville, New York, by throwing back mini bottles of gin and eating three bags of peanuts. When he exited the plane and grabbed his stuff, he was out of the airport and shielding his eyes from the glare. He saw the deputy right away. He was tall and thin, young, looking like some kid just stepping out of his senior year of high school.

"You the Ghostbuster?" Deputy Urinal asked.

"That's me. You recognized me?"

"Yeah, from a video I watched waiting for you. You do good work, it looks like."

"I try."

They were in the deputy's squad car, leaving the freeway and taking the winding route to Amityville. Most of the drive was full of beautiful woods bunched up against the shoulders of the road, and a few homes flecked meadows and farmland. The town itself was a small piece of the state, sitting on a rough oval-shaped spit of land abutting a rocky coast. It had the pleasant feeling of a place worth visiting during early summer or late fall. Very quaint, with a Main Street and buildings practically smashed together. Behind the business quarter were the homes, spreading up into the hills.

"You got a pretty town here."

"On the outside, sure. It's beautiful—postcard quality," Deputy Urinal said, hanging a left away from Main and shooting down the next right, heading for the precinct. "But inside, lurks evil."

"I just find it so hard to believe—"

"Well you better start believing, Ghostbuster, because those toilets . . ." Urinal calmed his voice and took a few breaths, changing up the route and hooking left. "Those toilets are dangerous. They've killed a lot of people."

"Toilets? I was told there was only one."

"Yeah, now . . . but before . . . it was awful."

"Tell me about it if you want."

"I don't think I can. It's classified."

Urinal guided them into a parking spot. "Leave your stuff, Ghostbuster, we're just going to meet the chief real quick. He wanted you here before we headed to the house."

Greg and Urinal were walking up the corridor that took them to Chief Balls's office. On the way, Greg noticed the darting glances of the other officers, as if they were afraid or maybe confused. It was hard to tell. The atmosphere of the place could be pinned as a grave.

"This way, Ghostbuster."

"It's Greg. You can call me Greg if you wish."

"Okay, Ghostbuster. Just inside here."

Urinal knocked and a gruff voice from inside barked, "Come in."

Urinal led the way, bidding Greg to follow and take a seat.

"Thank you."

Chief Balls gave him the once-over, then pulled a Winston from his pocket and lit up. "So, the famous

Ghost Man is sitting in front of my desk. I'm going to make this brief: you are a guest here. You will follow the law as everyone around here does. If you think for one second that you're above it, I'll loop the rope around your ass and have you hanging."

"Is . . . is that a threat to kill me?"

"Not at all, Ghost Man. Just a bit of lingo." But the fire was in Balls's eyes and you could never tell if the man was joking or not. "Now, you'll be working at the infamous Amityville House. And that will be your lodging, too, clear? The mayor wants this taken care of fast. He gave us three weeks, but I want you out in forty-eight hours. You find that goddamn ghost and turn him to dust."

Greg cleared his throat. "Technically, the poltergeist will not 'turn' to dust. It will either be expelled back to the spirit world or be a puddle of ectoplasm on the ground. Which I haven't seen before."

"Enough with the technicalities, Ghost Man. I don't give a good goddamn if you have to vacuum that pecker or spray him with some poison. Do whatever the hell it takes to get rid of it. Do you have everything you'll require?"

Greg nodded, about to say he did, but Balls cut him off at the nod.

"Good. Now Deputy Urinal will drive you and your toys out to the house. Dismissed. Oh, but before you go, I have to remind you." Balls leaned forward, his heavy elbows warping the oak surface of the desk. "Forty-eight hours, Ghost Man. You better wave your magic wand or do whatever trickery you have up your sleeve."

"And what if I can't do it in the time you request?"

"Ain't a request. You'll do it, and that's all there is to it."

"Look, I can't just 'do' these things. Sometimes it can take time. I might need those three weeks."

Balls blew a cloud of smoke out of his mouth and rubbed his temple. "Mayor Dump says that's okay. But I'm telling you it isn't. I don't want a bunch of weirdos coming into town once they learn you're here—because they will. Just get the shit done as fast as you can. Deputy? Get this Ghost Man out of my office."

"Yes, sir, Chief!"

On their way out, Greg again couldn't help but notice the glares from the officers in the building. They looked at him the same way Balls was eyeing him—like he was an invader into their beautiful little community.

SEVEN

Once Deputy Urinal said his goodbye and blew down the road over the speed limit, Greg shut the door behind him and just listened. He stood there in the foyer, opening his senses and getting the feel of the place. This was routine for him. The same way he started all of his assignments. First, he cased the joint, taking himself on a little tour and exploring the rooms and hallways, alcoves and corners, the basement and attic. Whatever there was to investigate, he swept it.

The Amityville house was big—two stories, wide and long. It had five bedrooms and two bathrooms, one huge kitchen annexed with a dining room, and opening from there was the living/family room. All bigger than the last. The place was still furnished in some parts, and others were bare and empty. It seemed whoever was tasked with cleaning up the place had figured it wasn't worth their time.

Or maybe they had been spooked. It was hard to say.

On the way over, Deputy Urinal said they had just cleaned up the remains of two squatters who were killed in violent toilet attacks. It was almost laughable to think about, but Greg wasn't laughing. As comical as the situation was to him, he emptied his laughter on the flight over. He was plumb out.

The deputy left him the squatter case photos and Greg glanced at these only briefly before setting them in his bag during his exploration.

His initial impression of the house left him scratching his head.

As experienced as he was in the field, no immediate readings were flicking at his noggin. No faint traces of a haunting, none of those weird smells he associated with the phantasmal. The place was empty. Just some old house needing restoration and a paint job. When he looked at the toilet—both of them—they were seemingly innocent porcelain models without a vapor of the weird. He ran a check of their sides from floor to lids. There was nothing off about them, and the flushing power was wonderful. Strong enough to suck down the mightiest of loads. Hell, maybe even strong enough to suck a puppy down the pipe.

Satisfied he'd covered each square of the house, he brought his phone out, logged into his channel, and hit the <LIVE> button. "Hey everybody, it's Greg G Allin from *Greg, The Ghost Hunter*. A little while ago, I was sunbathing poolside when I received a frantic phone call from the Amityville Chief of Police requesting my assistance in ridding one of their houses of a poltergeist. Or . . . and I'm sorry if I'm smiling . . . a toilet. Yes, folks, a toilet. A killer toilet, which supposedly killed two squatters in this very house not a week ago. Exciting, right?"

Keeping the camera on him, he took a walk through the house, showing off various rooms and hallways, everything he'd be working with during his stay and the eviction of this killer spirit.

"Now I'm not sure what level of poltergeist we're dealing with, but I will say it has to be a violent one to actually *kill* people. And from what I've been told, this isn't the first time. This is some seriously bad juju. But you know me, I'm Greg, The Ghost Hunter, and I get results. There isn't a ghost, ghoul, zombie, vampire, or alien monster that I can't dispel or throw out of existence," he joked. "I don't have all my gear with me, just the basics, but it will be enough for this job—that I'm certain."

Subscribers were filling the chat, poking questions at him.

"No, sorry, Sandra, Chuck won't be with me this time. I'm riding solo on this mission." He smiled and then continued. "Yes, I know he was a hit with you lovely ladies last time."

He scrolled to the next post: a contributor had just slid him fifty bucks as a tip. "Thank you for the high roll, Dustin87. To answer your question, no, I've never heard of Amityville except that the town was in the title of a movie. I don't watch horror, though. Haven't since I was a small kid. Sorry I can't help you."

Another tip dinged his account and he found the disburser. "TennesseeHotMILF. Well, if that isn't the best name I've seen in a long time. Yes, I'm wearing underwear, why do you ask?" A number was flashing on his screen. "Oh damn. I'm sorry, people. I'm going to have to put this LIVE on pause. I ask you to please have patience, and I'll return shortly and take you to the attic."

He thumb-swiped the green dot. "This is GG Allin."

"I know who you are, and that's why I'm calling! This is Mayor Dump—yes, *the* Mayor Dump. I've just learned the chief failed to inform me of your arrival. Typical. Well it doesn't matter, I suppose, so excuse me if my blood pressure is showing through my words. I don't care what the chief told you, that forty-eight hours crap is bullshit! Balls forgets that *I'm* in charge here, not him. I don't give a shit about his position any more than I do about yours. You're here on a job. You are being paid good money out of the town's coffers, and I expect results!"

"I assure you, Mayor Dump, that I don't leave a place until the spirits have vacated the property."

"That's good because that's why you're here." His voice took on a slight whisper with an edge. "Did the chief mention anything about a raid? Or anything else that he might have failed to notify me about?"

"No, no raid, Mayor. He just told me two squatters had been murdered recently in the Amityville H—"

"He revealed that to you?! I oughta . . . Goddamnit! He'll be hearing about this." There was a deep sigh before he continued. "Forgive me, I'm trying to remain calm, but I just find it irks me terribly when the chief starts shooting off his mouth."

"I don't think he did anything wrong, Mayor. It's actually quite beneficial to learn as much as I can about the toilet and the deaths associated with it."

"You do, do you?"

"Sure. It helps me to communicate with the . . . toilet."

"Whatever works, then that's fine with me. Just get rid of that thing, Greg. I can't have it here anymore. Tourist season . . . you hear me? TOURIST SEASON!"

"What about it?"

"Money, you fool! It brings in loads of money, and this town is in serious need of funds, if you haven't noticed."

"Whatever you say, but I thought the town was well taken care of. Everything looks new to me."

"It does, does it?"

"Yeah, very quaint and peaceful."

"That's how you feel, do you?"

"Yes, I do."

"All right, Ghost Hunter, whatever your name is again. But I'm watching you. I want that demon out of that house! Do whatever you need to do, but get that monster out of there before it spreads again!"

The phone clicked before Greg could ask what he meant by that last remark.

Flicking back to LIVE, Greg saw there were now dozens of people sitting in chat waiting for him to come back. "Wow, there's a lot more people in here now. I just got off the phone with the mayor of the town, and you're not going to believe this guy's name. You all ready for this? It's Mayor Dump! Yes, Dump, as in 'taking a dump.' Yeah, I see you're laughing same as I was when I first heard it. But bypassing that, he's adamant about getting this place rid of spirits. So that's what we're going to do for him. And that's what we always do, right, my fellow ghost enthusiasts?"

A bunch of smiling and laughing emotes flew up the screen.

"Okay, I'm going to get my gear settled in, and when I finish, I'll give you an update on my next move. Until then, stay spooky!"

———

Mayor Dump watched the whole stream. "That sonofabitch made a fool out of me on LIVE . . . what is this? Television or something? Whatever it is, all those goddamn people were there when he made fun of me! If he wasn't clearing out the Amityville House, I'd string him up by his balls! That's what I'd do. That slick cocksucker."

Fiddling with his fingers, he leaned back and stared out the window. The sky was darkening, going from daylight blue to bruise purple. The shadows were coming out to play now, and the whole town would soon be flooded over with them. It was going to be a long night wondering how that asshole was going to get this thing done.

And Mayor Dump, well, speaking of dumps, his butthole puckered and a faint whiff of what was coming sprung into his nostrils.

———

Chief Balls cracked a smile while smoking a Winston. "If I didn't think he was an idiot, I might invite him out for a beer." Balls thought it a hoot that Greg threw the mayor's name out there and joked about it. Seeing the responses from the people watching made it that much better.

End of shift was coming up so he took his feet off the desk, ashed his cigarette, and left the office, hitting the light on his way out.

Outside, stars were starting to cut through the blackening sky and a wind was rolling up the road, coming in off the Atlantic. A chill was in the air. He was in a car, lighting up another Winston, wondering if, in the morning, they'd have to shovel out another corpse from the Amityville House.

EIGHT

Setting up his gear was easy enough. Since throwing his anchor on vacation, he left most of it at home. Most, but not all. In his way of thinking, he should never go away empty-handed. You just never knew when a call for another job would come ringing in. That's the way it worked. At the most inopportune moments, the damn phone started chiming, and he was all for it. Even when he was getting a stiffy looking at that broad by the pool, he instantly switched himself over to work mode when he answered the call from the chief.

Balls, what a name. And the Mayor Dump and Deputy Urinal.

Three comical given names, but not one of them had any sense of humor to back it up. They saw nothing funny about anything. In fact, it seemed everyone he had run into left a lot to be desired in the smiling department.

Strange was one word for it.

An hour slipped by fast when setting up his gear, which was, essentially, a few small cams. Normally, he'd like everything on him, and if he required more, then he'd shoot a call to Ron, his buddy back home, to priority mail it to him.

But as it was, he wasn't so sure there was a problem here. Not a paranormal one anyhow. Usually, when entering a house, that house gives off a cold shoulder, throwing a bunch of phenomena at him. So far, he hadn't run into anything out of the ordinary. He had been in some houses where he instantly felt not welcomed. That his very presence was a violation of sacred ground, and he paid for this. Let him tell you if he has a few hours to spare. In one such instance, he was upstairs in a house, exploring for what the owners of the place called "eerie slime bleeding out of the wall." Well he happened to catch a glimpse of that substance—tiny rivers fed by a source growing angrier with his intrusion. Next thing he knew, he was caught in a fucking maelstrom of pressure blowing out of the wall, taking huge chunks of plaster and blasting it right at him. When he finally managed to find an exit, he was covered from hair to boot tip in a purple gelid coat of slime.

That was just one instance.

Greg could sit you down and rap your ear off for days. He had too many stories of different dangers. But one thing he never saw was an actual manifestation. He'd seen vapors and things like smoke floating through walls, but he had never actually seen a full-blown collection of particles solidify and cut his mind white with terror.

Not yet anyway.

Instead of going LIVE this time, he walked the house on his own. Really paying attention to what he would be working with. He went to every room and sat down in there, set his watch for ten minutes, and then moved on. He spent thirty minutes in the attic and fifteen in the basement—the only place he was feeling really uncomfortable. In each bathroom, he waited a combined count of nearly an hour.

Nothing.

No demons, ghosts, or killer toilets.

Killer toilets. This was a first, and his followers would be out of their minds laughing about it. And he was, too, mostly on the plane and some on the Uber ride to the airport.

Coming back into the living room, his official HQ for the duration, he sat down on the couch that was left behind, kicked his feet up on the cracked coffee table, and went through his notifications, swiping and clearing them. Responding to a few.

From his broadcast earlier, he had made quite the intake: $347.85.

More than enough to cover my last outing at the bar. He giggled.

"Guess I'll run a quick LIVE for the channel and tell the people the real work begins tomorrow." He said this, knowing it was the best course of action. Sometimes, a house could be incredibly violent to him, and other times, like now, there wasn't so much as a peep. He figured he'd sleep light and see how it went. Should anything occur during his rest, then he'd hit the <LIVE> button and start his magic.

"Okay, I'm dropping in for a quick note." Already, the chat was stacking with numbers. "I have my equipment set up and tested, and everything is functioning. I did another walk around the place and still didn't detect anything unusual. So, for the rest of the night, I'm going to remain silent and see what happens. No, don't worry, DomGhost81, if anything pops off, I'll be back. And everything will be recording while I'm asleep. But for now, ghost hunters, I'm out for the night. Peace!"

He winked and cut the feed.

He made sure his charger was juicing his phone and set it down on the table. He sighed and got comfortable on the couch. "If something is here, I'll know it soon."

How right he was.

NINE

In his dream, the girl from the pool was there. Not *in* the pool this time, but out of it, stripping to the skin and walking toward him like he was the perfect camera angle and she was the model. She pushed her breasts out to him, bit her lower lip, and flashed a pair of bedroom eyes that could ignite a volcano to burst. She worked the belt off his pants in one fluid motion, whipping it out of the loops and snapping it at her side.

Greg swallowed, wondering what she had in mind.

She brought the belt up with her other hand and bit down on the rough leather, working it slowly back and forth across her tongue. Down below, in that spot between his legs, there was a stirring and tickling. He felt the blood rushing up into his penis, inflating it, filling it to capacity where it rose fully erect, engorged and ready.

She cast the belt aside and lowered in a crouch, sliding her hand down his length, opening her mouth—

Then she bit the damn thing off. Ripped it free and swallowed it the way a duck swallows a meal. Blood was flying in her face. She let her mouth fall open to catch the delightful crimson fountain, suckering her lips over the base of what remained of his penis. She sucked him dry, literally. She inhaled his blood like a kid sucking the last drops of his cherry slushie. Greg was in full horror mode, leaning back and wagging his hips to dislodge the parasitic bitch leeching his blood.

But it was impossible. She fused to him, her lips welded just above his balls, which went the way of popped grapes, now hanging there like two skin tags covered in pubes. He pounded his fist on her head, bashing and bashing, but it was like trying to put a dent in a stone. She was making some internal vacuuming noise and the next thing he knew, Greg was withering, his skin flaking, his bones mushing into slime, his face going waxy before it ran right off the skull like a blast of water. His eyes were next, both boiling and then shooting off like corks popping from champagne bottles.

Then—

Greg woke up, pawing at his face, kicking his feet, and twisting his head right and left, breathing hard. "A dream. Jeez, just a dream."

A nightmare for sure. No dream was ever so horrible.

Sitting up and wiping the sweat off his face, he instantly checked his phone and saw a host of notifications piled up. This made him feel better, taking the dream from his memory and smothering it from existence. His eyes squinting from the glare, he swiped away the SPAM and checked off those more pertinent. With that taken care of, he felt the need to unburden his bladder.

He got to his feet, slapping his cheeks gently with both hands.

Then stopped.

No bodily movement, just his eyes, scanning slowly right and left, then upward to the ceiling. A noise . . . sounded like someone moving around upstairs, then another just down the hall. Thinking quickly, he reached into his bag beside the couch and pulled out the flashlight. With its beam lancing a path open in the darkness, he felt mildly emboldened. Left without its light, he had a feeling the nightmare beast of a woman would show herself. In some cleft, corner, maybe a shadow, she would emerge and run at him like he tripped the catch on a spring-loaded monster at a carnival spook house.

Taking light steps forward, he entered the hallway and paused, running his light up and down, listening. When nothing tickled his ears, he continued, pacing slowly, then swinging the light into the kitchen. Again, he allowed his breathing to relax and opened his ears.

He heard the wind playing outside but nothing else, just the silence of being alone in a big house. He turned aside and walked the hall, coming to the end and panning both left and right, seeing nothing amiss.

Movement just behind him turned him around, throwing his light down the hall. His heart was rattled because that sound was anything but normal. It sounded like footsteps, only running. A scurrying sound like someone didn't want to get caught. As he stood mute and resigned to his position, again he heard footsteps—going up the stairs now—as if they were taking their time, testing each step.

Thump . . . Thump . . . Thump . . .

I should have my phone, damn it. Why wasn't I thinking? This might be the day I actually see something worthy of recording!

Yeah, Greg might have gotten a chill or two, but he wasn't spooked entirely. This wasn't his first dalliance with the dead and departed. Only this time, there was something really off here. The beat of the heels and balls of the feet going up the steps was new. It sounded, if anything, like a real person coming upstairs.

Maybe someone is messing with me.

That was a real possibility and it wouldn't be the first time he'd experienced the displeasure of running into a couple of assholes out to make his life hell. One time, he caught a couple dressed up in Halloween costumes with plastic knives trying to put a scare in him. They succeeded, but he had the last laugh when something inside of him went primal and his fists did the dirty work his mouth couldn't put into words. He checked one with a right hook and took the other one off of his feet with a left, sending him crashing into a wall where he slid down like a wet turd thrown against glass.

After that, he had a few more. Most of these were fans of the show, trying to spice things up a pinch. But Greg, though grateful for his viewers/subscribers/fans, was steaming. While many people thought he was just bullshitting for money, he was the real deal. He was here to make the world safe from malevolent spirits, to free those entrapped by some elemental vise. And he had done so several times. But when people decided to enhance his broadcast with silly pyrotechnics and cheap Halloween rubber things, it made *him*—not them—look like a fool.

So if this was someone fucking with him now, he might just go ahead and let his fists do the talking. He was back in the living room and heading toward the staircase. He stopped at the bottom and winged the beam upward. Nothing was captured in the light.

"If anyone is up there who thinks it's funny to interfere with my work, show yourself. I'm not in the mood to deal with this crap. I'll give you five seconds."

He counted down in his head, and a whole lot happened during that time.

Outside, the wind howled and threw gusts against the house, battering the windows with sticks and yard waste. A hundred—no, hundreds of feet were pounding on the ceiling and running ghostly up the steps. Laughter echoed and whispers struck his ears, cutting up his spine like knives.

Then silence.

His heartbeat was off the charts and all he could do was stare, bested by . . . something. Something like he'd never experienced before.

Something evil.

TEN

Greg had plenty of time to think before the sun finally showed itself and punched the night back with its red, misty pouring of warmth through the windows and into the house. That simple celestial gesture made him feel good and chased away some of the chill left on his bones. And yes, Greg, The Ghost Hunter was chilled by the experience. In all of his days flinging ghosts off the earth, he had never faced something so eerie. Sure, he'd seen funny, amorphous shadows, heard cackling in the night, the blow of arctic winds in cellars, and seen eyes the color of fresh blood hiding up in the corners of attics, but nothing so volatile as what he'd experienced just a few hours before.

Since then, all had been quiet, except his heartbeat, which was ticking up in speed the more he reflected back on it. And the nightmare, of course.

He brought his channel up and gave it a look. He had a lot of messages cheering him on in his hunt and others asking if he was okay. Deciding he'd better respond because the patience of his fans wears thin, he thumbed the **<LIVE>** button. Running a hand through his hair, he started.

"Gooood morning, fellow ghost hunters! It's Greg, The Ghost Hunter to report on some strange occurrences last night. First off, let me say thank you to all who checked in with me during the night. Your support goes a long way in my book. Anyway, after I set up my equipment,"—which got him instantly thinking about checking the camera feeds—"I had quite the visitor, or visitors. Let me say, at first, I thought it could be another intruder, and those who have been with me long enough remember my run-ins with crazies. But this was no intruder, nothing human. How do I know? Well, you'll just have to take my word for it. I'll give you a breakdown of what occurred . . ."

After he laid it out as crystal as he remembered it, he continued. "So that leads me to believe something very evil is here. I can't say what it is exactly, but I know it doesn't want me here. I guess it's only a matter of time before it shows itself and that's what worries me. Egon-GhostBuster asks if I was scared when it happened. Thank you for the gratuity, Egon, much appreciated, buddy, and yes, I had a mild scare." He actually had a severe scare and was too afraid to admit that fact. Greg was solid as adamant. If he showed any vulnerability, he might lose some subscribers. So, instead, he kept his vigilance about him. "But it was a tiny chill. Nothing serious. The day that Greg, The Ghost Hunter gets really scared, you'd better start worrying. Okay, I've cleared that. Today I'll spend doing an intricate check of the house—especially the bathrooms. I'll be combing the basement first, then working my way up to the attic."

A knock on the door brought his face away from the phone.

"Excuse me, ghost hunters, I have a visitor—no, nothing scary—well, maybe!" He paused the broadcast and affixed his charger back into the phone. Going to the door, he unlatched the bolt and chain and swung it open.

"Ghost Man, I've dropped by to hear some progress."

Chief Balls was standing there with his thumbs hooked into his duty belt, his aviator glasses as dark and foreboding as his voice. He was chewing on something and his Stetson was hiked off his forehead.

"Oh, Chief, nice to see you, but—"

"Bullshit. Now step aside, I'm coming in."

Greg opened the door fully and did as the chief demanded. "Sorry the place is a mess," he joked.

"Funny."

Greg closed the door and followed the chief, who paused every sixth step and stared up at the ceiling and floor, scanning as if looking for something in particular. He took his shades off, folded them, and placed them in his breast pocket. Taking his hat off, he set it on the coffee table. He took one glance at Greg's gear and made a face. "How was your first night?"

"Well . . ." Greg told him exactly how it went.

"Sounds about right. Folks around here say they hear weird shit coming from this house on certain nights. They say they even catch eyes staring out at them from the windows. Shadows, too," he said, spitting on the floor. "They see moving shadows—like ink blots, someone reported to me once. They said, first it was thin as a wire up in one of the second-story windows, then it spread out like a pair of wings, and finally imploded, spraying the glass black, then fading. Pretty scary stuff, wouldn't you say?"

Greg nodded.

"I'm going to cut the convo to a few questions now. Can you tell me what haunts this place exactly?"

"Not yet, no. But I should know something very

soon. This thing—whatever is here—it seems like it's everywhere in the house, and not just the toilet."

"Is that right, Ghost Man?

Sensing something hidden in his face, Greg pushed the conversation to a different angle. "Is there anything you can give me that can help here? Any history whatsoever?"

Balls smiled at Greg for a full minute before saying, "Long story, but I guess I can give you the bullet points."

Fingering out a slab of chew from his lip, Chief Balls tossed it to the floor and lit up a Winston. He went on to say that once upon a time, there had been several murders outside this house. Since then, all the toilet-related deaths have been centered at the Amityville House, killing off each subsequent owner. Entire families gone, *erased*, butchered in the bathroom by the toilet.

That wasn't much help, but Greg decided not to press the issue any further. Besides, he got a little info he could twist the right way. "So let me get this straight," Greg said, secretly taking his broadcast off pause. "You think there's some sort of demon or ghost or something like that in this town, jumping from toilet to toilet, and now it's here and doesn't seem to be going anywhere?"

"I'd say you retained the information correctly, Ghost Man."

"I can't say I've ever dealt with a toilet-jumping entity, but I'll handle it for you."

"Of course you will, because that's why you're being paid."

"Is there any other information you could give me? Anything you might have left out before I came here?"

Chief Balls smiled the way a corpse staring out of its casket does, then blew smoke out his nostrils. "Nothing."

"Okay then."

"I've said enough. It's just one of my duties as Amityville Police Chief to check on our famous Ghost Man. I think Mayor Dump has a thing for you. I mean, since you clowned him pretty good on your channel last night."

Greg smiled. "You saw that?"

"Surely I did. Just know, you're always being watched."

Whatever that meant. "Sure, I'll remember. Now I got a lot of work to do, Chief, so, if you wouldn't mind . . ."

"I respect that." He was out the door, dragging the smoke to the filter. "One last thing. If you go into town, lock this place up. I don't need anybody coming in here and getting themself killed."

"Sure thing."

Greg watched the chief get in his cruiser and pull away. He brought the phone to his face. "Creepy guy, huh?" he asked his viewers. The feed went up with laughing emotes and witty replies. "Anyway, guys and gals, I'm getting hungry and I think I should at least get something to eat before I start my day. I will check in soon! And in the meantime, stay spooky!"

ELEVEN

Jessica had been watching him for years now. And finally, he was on location just down the road. Not just a simple jogging distance or even a bus fare, but in her mind, he was down the road. One hundred and eighty-seven miles and some change, to be exact. But she wasn't about to let the gap separate her from what she wanted.

And that was Greg—Greg, The Ghost Hunter.

Yeah, she had some things in mind for Greg. One of which was to lay him down and pull his penis out. She wanted to stroke it and maybe wrap her lips around it. Once it got hard, she'd mount him, plug herself in, and hopefully get zapped creamily by his charge.

But would he agree to it? Or would he shove her aside and call the police, like her obsessions often had the gall to do?

Either way, she wasn't about to stop.

Especially now since she was in Amityville, walking across the lawn after exiting the passenger side of an Uber.

The house wasn't anything special. And like Greg, she wasn't getting any pings off this place. You see, Jessica was something of an amateur ghost hunter. After catching a season of Greg's channel, she decided she was going to do something like that. She even dropped a few thousand on some gear and trained herself how to sniff out ghosts. So far, she hadn't found anything. She even explored a few abandoned places known to be haunted.

What a dead end those had turned out to be.

Thing is, here at the Amityville House, she wasn't much interested in poking her nose in any ghost business. She brought her equipment, but that was a cover. She had other things in mind. Mostly taking Greg's pants down to his ankles and giving him a blow job that she hoped would make him fall in love with her.

Why? Because Jessica had butterflies over Mr. Right. That's what she called him. She didn't even know the man. Watched him regularly, but she didn't *know* him beyond the screen. That didn't matter. Not at all. She would love him and show him a side he would never resist or forget.

She prepared herself to see him. To actually see The Ghost Hunter!

She knocked.

Waited.

After a few more raps, she tried the knob.

The door swung inward.

She took a few measured breaths and entered.

She wasn't sure if she closed the door behind her or if it just closed on its own. In hindsight, what difference did it make? She was in the house of her obsession. And soon he would know love like he'd never known before.

"Uh, hello?"

Her voice carried through the house like wind chimes echoing off a breeze. She got a look at her surroundings and felt . . . comfortable. There was no presence, nothing evil or haunted about the place.

Greg said there was a tangible violation—an entity marking its territory here. But she wasn't getting that vibe. No, this place was warm, made her feel like she was walking through her grandparents' house. It had that cozy, welcoming feel to it.

"Uh, Greg . . . GG Allin? You here?"

Her voice swung back at her. The place was empty. Nothing here.

But!

His equipment was laid out there in the living room. "Oh my God."

She went over and touched it all, stroking his gear and smelling the couch where he'd said he slept. She could smell a manly odor rising off those fibers and it made her nipples hard.

"Oh my God, I'm actually *smelling* him!"

As she fondled his equipment like it was an extension of him, she stroked her vagina to wet.

"Greg," she called out, her voice bouncing off the walls. "I don't want to alarm you, but I'm here." She said this as if he should recognize her. Jessica was a big fan, after all—she regularly contributed to his tips and was always talking in the chat box. "I know this is weird, but I . . . I just needed to meet you. I'm sorry, but I can't help myself. Greg?"

She walked around. As far as she could tell, there was no one here. She felt sad about it. Maybe he was still out getting some food like he'd said.

She decided she would drop her things and wait for him. She reached into a side pocket of her bag, pulled out a candy bar, slid the wrapper down, and took a bite. As she did so, her eyes wandered around the place. She moved about freely, touching the walls and doors, exploring like someone in an alien place. She was upstairs when she felt her guts start to roil.

"Oh no, I think I ate too much chocolate."

She stuffed the candy into her pocket and checked the doors, finally finding the bathroom. She hesitated at first, remembering that the reason Greg was here was to investigate and purge the demon toilet monster.

"I'll be fine." She giggled.

Confident she would be, she traipsed over and lowered her panties, sat her pretty rump on the toilet, and let go with a piss. Ten or fifteen seconds later, she was wiping up her stuff when the toilet made a noise like an upset stomach. The water in the tank behind her started to rumble.

She felt the dread of hanging in the maw of some spirit beast. There was a feeling in her like she would soon snap in half, her bones crushed, blood shooting out in all directions. Carefully, she hiked up her panties and fastened her pants, slowly turning around and staring.

Just a toilet.

Nothing more. Just a plain old toilet and water stained a faint gold from her piss.

Shaking her head, she hit the flusher and that's when all hell burst on the scene.

The toilet extended out of the ground, shaping into an indescribable horror with a porcelain exterior full of hairline cracks and mottled and ophidian-like skin beneath. The toilet tank shattered into a face, its purple/red eyes flipped open, then lowered into neon slits glaring with hatred. A mouth split apart with a deafening roar of teeth flinging saliva ribbons. She cried out for Greg and fell back against the wall.

But it was too late. The toilet monster shot forward and took her in its mouth, sealing down to her waist and pulling her in half like hot taffy. From her hips exploded an ever-mounting surge of blood and viscera, a meat fountain that rose to the ceiling and showered the room red and sticky.

It took her into its pipe throat and flushed her down.

Then quickly, it finished her lower half, leaving only shards of bones jutting from two shoes on the floor.

TWELVE

Before leaving the house that morning, Greg checked the cameras he had installed the day of his arrival, and nothing was recorded from the previous night. Just a lot of fuzz and scratches. This irked him. Not that he expected to see anything floating across the footage or to discover the actual source of what made those pounding footsteps. What bothered him most was it appeared the cameras had weakened, as if something was working to drain their energy.

Needing to clear his head and think things through, he took a walk to town.

His quick sojourn to the heart of the coastal paradise garnered him little information about its citizens. From what he quickly scraped from the surface, this town's residents were a bit jumpy. Like there was something just out of sight, hanging around where it shouldn't be. Like a presence biding its time to manifest to an unholy degree. He found the locals standoffish, reluctant to speak past a few salutations. He was able to order his food from a sandwich shop but it was like talking to a drive-thru menu box.

The young lady behind the counter was a pretty twentysomething with long brown hair woven into a single thick braid down her back, bright green eyes the color of summer limes, and a button nose. She had the faintest curl of a smile on her lips when she saw him. But as he went to order, she shut down and became a deli automaton. She took his order fast, then just as fast, had the twelve-inch meatball sub shoved into his hands.

"Thank you," he told the pretty gal.

She looked at him like he was some alien, some invader in her town. Her lips went crooked with a frown and he noticed the rest of the employees had likewise twisted their countenances into sneers of disapproval.

He didn't stick around to reproach the strange situation. Instead, he turned his back to them and sauntered out into the fog and sunshine.

As he made his way up Main, he had a feeling he was not alone. He paused at an intersection and scanned each corner. Beyond the shy faces of the locals, he saw a police cruiser on the side of the road. Deputy Urinal was behind the wheel, eyeing Greg sharply. Like the barrel of a rifle, Urinal tracked Greg as he covered the rest of Main in slow footfalls, gazing every now and then at the myriad stores lined up over its multiple blocks. He ducked into a few of them and saw the cruiser rolling, then double-parked until he walked out.

He thought about asking the young Urinal what his malfunction was or why he thought it okay to track him like he was. The way Greg was feeling was confused. It was like he was a step away from being incarcerated. Or maybe there was something more sinister afoot.

Shrugging the nonsense from his shoulders, he left Main and wound his way up the fog-shrouded streets to the Amityville House. And the entire journey, he heard the motor of Urinal's cruiser rumbling behind him like a tiger with an empty belly.

Crossing the lawn, he turned and saw he was alone

again. Just him and the fog, a thick cloud of it shoving up against the house now. He could scarcely see three to five feet off the porch before a wall of mist smothered the town's sounds with echoes.

"Like a dream," he said to himself.

Because to him, yeah, at times, it did feel like he was the character in a dream or some morbid play. It was funny. There was an instance when he felt like the sacrifice for a backward town—a town clutching onto old superstitions of folkloric gods and demons. Maybe that's what this was about. They needed someone to offer blood to their god.

No, that was stupid.

This was about a haunted toilet.

Nothing more. And if he started catching and holding onto ideas floating from his mind, he was in deep shit.

Throwing the door open, he went inside and locked it behind him.

He stood in the foyer, breathing in the musty air, listening to a soundlessness that was almost too much. Gone was that audible piercing you often get with mute surroundings. It was just gone. There was a silence in this house akin to a tomb. The pure, black, terrible silence of outer gulfs, of the byways hanging in deep space. He slid the paper down on his sub and got to chewing, slurping out a big meatball that almost choked him. Taking a tour of the house, he noticed a difference that was not so much obvious as it was ethereal. An odor triggered scrunching his nose.

"What the heck is that smell?"

His nostrils continued to investigate, leading him from the ground floor up to the second. He came to the landing and let his nose latch onto the scent.

"This way, I think . . . "

Taking a big bite of his sub, he laid it on the banister and took his phone out, snapping it to YouTube. He flicked off the notifications bunching his screen, then immediately thumbed **<LIVE>**. "Hello there, ghost hunters, this is an emergency broadcast. After my uneventful stroll into town, I came back here and . . . I dunno, I'm feeling . . . strange. Not *me*, really, but something about the house. It's not right—not like it was when I left this morning." He panned the camera away from his face and showed his mounting number of viewers the hall he was walking. "Nothing weird so far, huh?" He flipped the phone around to highlight his face and narrative. "Yes, FatherFecal, that is a sub sandwich you saw on the banister; my feast was rudely interrupted by my current circumstances. But don't worry, I'll be chewing on it soon! Anyway, back to the feed. You see, I smelled this strange smell and now it's positively blistering my nostrils. I think it's coming from over there." He moved down the hall, taking each stride carefully. "Okay, I'm stopping right here." He showed the bathroom door. "I'm getting a real hot reading—or *feeling*, I should say, since I don't have my EVP detector with me—from this door. Yes, folks, it's the bathroom. I don't know what to expect when I open it, so . . . be prepared."

Touching the knob brought an instant shock to his fingertips.

"Ouch!" Like a biting static electricity. "That hurt. Let me try that again."

Using his shirt to cover his hand, he turned the knob, or at least, attempted to. He exerted more pressure. "It's really tight. Feels like it's been welded shut. Jeez."

A few more muscles thrown down his wrist and he managed to shift the knob. "Okay, I think I got it."

He gave it a hard crank to the right and it gave. The

door swung open on hinges like screaming fairies, "And here we are—"

The last word in his mouth trickled out in a tight, choking sob. The bathroom . . . it looked like a god-damn crime scene. Volumes of blood painted up all four walls and pooled on the tiles, forming a seal around the edges. The mirror, the ceiling, the bathtub—all were red and wet—streams of cruor oozing down the side of the tub, filling its depth to the rim.

"I . . . I don't know what—"

He couldn't think of how to carry on speaking.

The only piece of the bathroom that wasn't heaped in gore was the toilet. The thing was pristine. Fresh and shining—mint. Greg was overcome by a bad case of the shakes. It wound him up, causing his teeth to chatter. He ran a check of the floor and took a step back.

Snapped ankle bones jutting out of two purple shoes, blood crusted over the eyelets of the laces. "Chief Balls," he managed to utter quaveringly. "If you're watching this . . . Get down here now."

———

Mayor Dump had watched the whole thing from start to finish. He watched as Greg went LIVE and nearly lost his balance as the camera fumbled at the hideous bloodbath in the bathroom.

But Mayor Dump wasn't surprised. As much as he wanted to scream his mind loose, it couldn't get any more loose. Not with the amount of death he had seen over the duration of this demon toilet's occupation. It did startle his nerves a little, so he was on the phone to the chief.

"Balls, you get down to that house right now!"

"Keep your voice down, Mayor. I don't like scratchy

phone calls. Besides, I was watching just as you were. I've seen it. I'm on my way now."

"Good. And make sure this is the last kill, Balls. Tell Greg to expedite this entity to the grave! Hurry!"

Balls slapped the phone down. He grabbed his hat off the hook, hiked his holster, and was in his cruiser, cutting through the foggy streets, then pulling up to the Amityville House.

It was like something out of a storybook when you got to look at it. It made something inside dry up and pull at the old strings of youth. It could make the staunchest adult wither. With the way the fog was pouring against the exterior, the whole structure seemed an evil, blighted protrusion from the earth. Like it wasn't a house but a tumor—a malignant protuberance swelling out of a fracture in the soil.

Without announcing himself, he walked right in, calling out, "Ghost Man, I'm here."

Greg, bloodless-looking, startled Chief Balls when he came around the corner. "Upstairs, Chief. In all my years of doing this, I have never seen anything so horrible."

Balls, always with a standard Winston hanging off his lip, kept one thumb hooked in his belt and brought his other hand up to take away the cigarette. "Around here, Ghost Man, you'll learn this is just another day. I told you it was dangerous. Any moment now, the proper crew will be here to clean this up. And when that happens, you'll stay out of the way."

Greg was fine with those terms. He had seen enough of the slaughter.

Balls detected something. "You okay there, Ghost Man?"

"A little shaken up. And my viewers too. They weren't ready for that, that, that awfulness," Greg stammered.

"I figured as much. I was going to say, you look like you've seen a ghost." He laughed.

Oh, like he hadn't heard that one a million times. "Clever."

"You ain't thinking of popping smoke from my town, are you?"

"Greg, The Ghost Hunter never backs down," he said with a lack of conviction. "No matter what." Then a flash of the gore upstairs made him swallow some bile. "Up there, it was bad, but I have a job to do, and I'll do it."

Balls nodded, appreciative of Greg's resolve. "That's what I wanted to hear. A man who is not afraid to shoo away a ghost. Because that is what we're working with here, *right?*"

Greg gave it some thought before answering. A ghost? He wasn't so sure. A pissed-off ghost? Likely. But still, it could have been something more deadly. A *real* demon. "I'm not sure what we're dealing with. But what I do know, is it's a deadly, irritated entity."

Keeping the conversation minimal, Balls nodded and drew off his cigarette. "I hear the cars rolling up now. Keep yourself out of their way."

Greg made a mental note to tell that guy to fuck off when he got through with this job. Balls acted like none of this bothered him. Or maybe it did and he was just covering it over with a small-town hard-ass exterior. Either way, it disturbed Greg plenty. To see the entity's handiwork was a gut punch. It curled up his faculties and gave them a real scare.

Still, he would not be swayed. If the thing was going to kill him, it would have already found a way. In the meantime, he apologized to his feed. Telling them he had no idea what he was going to find. Most were shaken up, but there were a few dissecting every angle and reporting how elaborate the effects were, saying it was just bullshit to spike ratings.

Stupid fucks.

The crew came inside, paying him no attention. As they worked, Greg sat back and checked on his earnings for the month, a simple thing to distract him. And when the mop upstairs started sloshing up the blood and the smell of ammonia and death came down those stairs like an entity itself, Greg stepped outside and helped himself to one of his own cigarettes.

"It's going to be a long night."

THIRTEEN

The police and emergency personnel were thorough and effective. They didn't leave the faintest trace of blood or disaster in the bathroom. The way they got it to sparkle like a bathroom cleaner commercial surprised Greg. He figured, with that amount of death spilling over, there would be some faint scent lingering in the air. But there hadn't been. Nothing at all. No vapor that wasn't the ammonia fumes of a deep clean.

Once they packed up and evacuated the grounds, Balls stood by, again, pressing a glare into Greg's eyes. "You be careful, Ghost Man. You just never know when nature calls. You might find yourself oblivious to the danger and go stumbling in there to relieve yourself. Only you'll be relieving more than just your bladder. You read me?"

Greg hadn't the time or the patience to listen to the chief, who seemed to love hearing the inflection of his own voice.

"Now sleep tight, Ghost Man. If you need anything . . . I'll be watching."

Greg punched the <LIVE> button once Balls pulled off the property.

"Sorry about the long intermission, people. I had to

deal with Chief Balls longer than I would have liked. I'm sure you understand." A vertical row of agreement splashed the screen. "And, again, I apologize for the . . . you know." Sitting back on the couch, Greg continued. "As you all know, this place is haunted. We remember the first night, right? And now this . . . death. I'm not sure I'm dealing with any kind of spirit I've had a hand in dispelling in the past. This is something completely different. I'm going to have to be more cautious with my approach. And if you know me at all, that is not my normal routine. I'm a bit disturbed, truthfully. I've never seen such bodily destruction and so much blood before. But I have to remind myself that not all ghosts are spirits looking for a door. Some like their new surroundings a little too much. And with this one,"—Greg looked around as he panned the camera to follow his eyes—"this one is going to be a challenge. What will happen? We don't know. First things first, I need to explore some more. Spend more time around the bathrooms. Maybe try to reach out to this entity. With some daylight still showing, I think I might try that soon. I don't think I'll be doing much during the night. At least, not until I know more. Tomorrow I'm going to try and find some more information about this. I tried the Internet earlier, but I had no success. Anything I did find related to a toilet demon in Amityville had been scrubbed—the links were bad. So, looks like I'll be stepping into the shoes of a detective too."

Greg sighed and pulled a cigarette from a pack on the coffee table. "Yeah, old habit. I carry cigarettes—Camel Reds—with me but hardly ever feel the need to smoke them. After today, though, I'm pining. I'll check in later when I'm ready to investigate further. Until then, be ready for anything! Greg, The Ghost Hunter, out."

———

Greg couldn't remember passing out.

But the voice blaring over him, causing his lips to flick open wide, confused him with the image of a man leaning above him.

"Uh, wait— Who are you?"

Those were the first words off Greg's lips, and they were well-placed. As confused as he was with the man, he was even more befuddled at the dude's sleepwear.

"You're, you're wearing pajamas?"

Another perfectly placed question. The guy was wearing a pair of silk pants and matching top—blue with spots of red. He was of medium height, with dark eyes, a bald and shining dome, and a face not too happy seeing Greg enjoying a nap on the couch.

"What are you doing here, man?"

"*Me?*" Greg asked, finally sitting up and keeping his distance. "What are *you* doing here? I was told nobody was allowed in here. And how did you get in? I locked the doors."

"Don't try feeding me bullshit, Greg. This is my goddamn house and you better get the hell out of it right now before I call the police! And take your shit with you."

"Wait a minute, wait a minute . . ." This was almost too much. Greg had been yanked out of a deep nap by this pajama-wearing lunatic, and now the guy was telling him it was *his* house and Greg wasn't welcome. "This is nobody's house. What are you talking about?"

"Oh, let me guess, Mayor Dump and Chief Balls told you that, didn't they?"

"Yes, but I walked through this place multiple times, and there—"

"Well," the man sneered, "you must have forgotten

an important corner because this is my abode, friend, and you are trespassing!"

"Trespassing?"

"Do you not understand the meaning of the word?"

"No, I get it. But—"

"Enough of the buts. Listen, this is my house, and I don't want you in here, okay?" You take down your little cameras, gather your gear, and get to moving now. Because if you don't, I'm gonna get really pissed off."

"Wait, please just give me a minute to say something."

"Let me guess, you're going to say Chief Balls and Dump hired you to chase the spirits away from here, right?"

"Yes—"

"That's the line they feed to all the idiots they send here on the same errand. You aren't the first!"

Craftily, Greg hit the **<LIVE>** button on his camera. The angle was off, but it showed the man clear enough. "What do you mean? I was told this was the first time. Do you mind if I ask your name?"

"My name? You want to know my goddamn name in my goddamn house?"

"Please, I do. My name is Greg—"

"I know that, smart guy! Remember? I said it already!"

"How— Oh, you must have seen me on YouTube."

"YouTube? I don't have time to watch that stupid shit. Now are you going to get out of my house? Or am I going to have to make you?"

At first, Greg thought the guy wasn't going to wait for an answer, then he crossed his arms as if waiting.

"Okay . . . I'll leave if that's what you want, but—"

"But again?"

"*But*, what if I don't leave?"

"If you don't? Then you'll see how mad I can get. Screw the cops, I'll take care of you myself!"

Just as Greg prepared himself to grapple with this obviously confused interloper, his reactions were slowed as the man started shivering around like a spider molting its skin, as his flesh became a synthetic sleeve set with a rippling of tiny waves, slowly webbed with creases which broke open in seams of blue light, widening out until they ran from the bones like blood, splatting the floor in pasty clumps. But it wasn't bones showing, but pipes—silver pipes and plastic tubing, a porcelain exoskeleton over a frame of sewer pipes as translucent as crystal, clogged with piss and shit and blood. Greg reeled back, choking on a scream, and was blasted with wind as the thing bellowed, "I'M SEBAST-IAN! AND THIS IS MY HOUSE!"

Then whatever flesh remained sluiced to the floor as a combination of blood and piss and shit vomited from its mouth, slamming into Greg, lifting him off his feet to touch the ceiling with his head. The rancid cocktail rushed down his mouth, distending his belly—

And then the toilet monster was no more.

Greg was cowering and shivering, wiping at himself. But there was nothing there. Not even a bead of sweat. In fact, it was quite cool in the house, and a hint of sunshine pressed against the window panes.

It was eerily silent.

Greg checked out the camera to report to his viewers.

But the phone was off. Turned off completely. The battery drained.

"No, I had just turned it on . . ." He heard the toilet flush upstairs and some laughter not even remotely close to human.

Fourteen

Nighttime came swinging over Amityville, sucking away the colors and blanketing blackly and terribly over houses, businesses, and bay. Shadows, profound and engulfing, and in their voids pounded demon hearts. The town was a fucking tomb for a nightmare with the lid thrown open wide.

"This is the second time I've tried to go LIVE tonight, fellow hunters. I explained to the earlier crowd what happened, and if you missed it, I'm sorry, but you'll have to wait until the video uploads and posts to my channel to get more information. What I will say about it, and I'll keep this brief,"—Greg felt his fingers shake again—"is that the presence here is pure evil. And I've never confronted such a power before. I might not be strong enough to expel this one. But, in the same manner that I've dealt with these things before, I will continue with my best efforts. I have to remain strong for this one. Earlier, I was attacked in my sleep—I think I was dreaming. Yes, it was a dream. It had to be. A man claiming to reside here, Sebastian, said I was trespassing before he became . . ." Greg wanted to laugh but didn't dare. "He became a toilet monster. Human skin, then a toilet monster. I don't know, people. This is a crazy one. And as night is here, I'm going to stay awake rather than sleep. I've had enough of that for today. Right now, I'm going to bring out my crystal and my crow feather—if you know me at all, you know I always have these with me for protection. I just hope these work magic as they have in the past."

"I'm going to keep the lights on from now on too. I'm going to really project my strength, and as an empath, I'm going to seek out this *thing* and see what we can do about dislodging it, not only from this home but from this planet!"

He shut the broadcast down after saying his goodnight to the viewers, then held his position, standing there, exerting his power to the house. He wanted it to know he wasn't going to be pushed around anymore. He was here to do a job, and he would do it. The only thing that would stop him, was death. And though he feared it hacking at him from some shadowed corner, he could not let the possibility defeat him. He was The Ghost Hunter, not a scammer or a scoundrel; he was a warrior of light, and he would battle this poisonous spirit.

————

With help from his EVP detector (for those who don't know, it's an electronic device able to pick up sounds and voices not hooked into human frequencies), Greg took his first steps through the ground floor. He poked around spots in the living room and finding nothing out of place, he moved into the kitchen. He took his time, going up and down, floor to ceiling, cabinet to counter, and under the sink, swaying in and out around the pipes. When no readings registered on the EVP detector, he took his leave and traced up and down both the dining room and hallways.

Now to the ground floor bathroom.

This was a more formidable task, and though the lights were on strong throughout the house, being that it was night, he still let one fact linger in his mind. This was the hour of the phantoms, which brought an unnerving squirm along his bones. Nevertheless, he hiked up his big boy pants, took a deep breath, and went in.

Immediately, the EVP detector picked up something. Whatever energy was present was pinging the device with static and pinpoint screeches. He eyed the place, swinging the EVP device high and low, and the lower it went, the more those screeches turned their volume high and shrill. It punched into his ears.

"I don't like that at all."

Though there were increases in EVP spikes, he wasn't feeling an overwhelming danger. He was certain if he lingered or spent any more time investigating, he would likely face whatever was here in its wrathful form, and this time it wouldn't be a dream.

Backing out, he noted the time and marked the readings on a pad and voice recorder app on his phone. Carefully backing his way out of the hall, he turned and faced the staircase, running his eyes up the steps to the second floor.

"Let's do this."

He took the stairs one at a time, sweeping without readings.

He made it to the landing and calmed himself down with a few steady breaths. For some reason, he was assailed with a bad feeling as he climbed those steps. He figured something slimy and fresh from a swamp of blood would show itself and leap onto him, take him tumbling down the steps to land broken and tangled, then fed into a maw with teeth like sharpened rib bones.

As it was, there was nothing, not even a cold spot on this floor.

He shook the heebie-jeebies out of his head and continued to the rooms.

The master bedroom was simple. Like the other rooms, this was empty but for some old boxes and 2x4s. No increase in EVP spikes, nothing. He left the doors open and made for the bathroom.

The dreaded bathroom where the tub of blood and death was discovered, where the toilet shined as if rubbed by a cloth and a bottle of Gel-Gloss. He felt a chill wing his back from his hip bones to the base of his skull. His heartbeat sped up high. He took the knob and twisted.

The door opened, and the smell of ammonia slapped him from inside.

Clean as ever. Pristine and wiped of blood . . . and death.

"Okay, Greg. You can do this. Go in there."

He did. He took in a gulp of air like he was fixing to leap off a high dive into a pool. He stepped in there and let it slowly escape his lungs. Still haunted by the sight and smell of the bathroom massacre, his fingers shook around the EVP detector as he cut the air in slow strokes, then lowered it to the toilet.

He was half-expecting to see the guy again, to see Sebastian with his pants down, smiling at him with a grin cut out with a knife, eyes gouged out and filled with toilet water. But nothing of the sort met his vision, and he was happy for that. Sweeping to the base of the toilet, going around the backside, hesitant of the lid lifting and a mouth or hand grabbing hold of him, he kept his eyes flicking up and down. He came away from the toilet when the EVP detector went wild with a shrill piercing, like a rape whistle, in his ears. It turned the device as hot as an oven-baked brick. He yelped as it burned his fingers, and the EVP detector hit the ground, wisps of smoke coming off of it.

He took his phone out and immediately snapped pictures while remaining cautious of the toilet. Without using his hands or skin in any way, he kicked the EVP device into the hallway and backed out as if in the sights of a gun barrel. Carefully, he shut the door, dreading a wave of cloaked wraiths leaping from the toilet and reaching after him.

He made an audible note with his phone. "It seems the real power is indeed coming from the toilets. But *why* is the question, and what can I do to remove the source?"

Deciding against exploring the attic and basement, as he figured there was nothing up or down there worth his time, he left the house with his flashlight and checked out the front, sides, and backyard.

The front yard was empty. No signs, no readings, just a lot of darkness and the cold bite of a sea wind gusting through town. As with the front, both flanks of the house were dead ends. Just shadows and moonlight. Now in the backyard, that's where things took a spin.

He was out there, cutting a swath of light in the shadows when the ground started to rumble. It started as a faint seismic wave, followed by a grumbling, as if Greg had hit a switch and popped off a series of detonations beneath. He stood still as a lamppost, keeping the beam of his light in one spot, watching as the grass around his feet and farther out started to boil like water, except for exactly where he stood. Sections of the lawn rose like balloon skin inflating with helium. Greg felt like running. He almost did, too, but the ground then flattened out as if nothing had happened, leaving him shaking and waiting for disaster.

When none occurred, he took his first step and froze.

A sound like a chainsaw starting up fried his nerves. But it wasn't a chainsaw, he realized after listening to its lowering report. It was . . . Well, it sounded like an ass ripping out a long, ghastly quiver of a fart. Greg felt the vibrations underfoot and worried for one moment that the ground would rip apart and suck him below, the entire descent wrapped in farts.

He swung his light in all directions, even up into the sky where the moon and stars stared down coldly. Around him, the sounds of farts increased, becoming one massive flatulent crackle, detonating as if a thousand assholes just let go with a year's worth of gas.

And speaking of gas, rising off the lawn was a thin veil of green vapor. It started as a mist, then steadily condensed into that of an opaque pea soup and lifted as high as his neck, completely inundating the lawn and as far as he could see—which wasn't very far, considering clouds of the greenish miasma were stinging his eyes. He was choking, feeling this feculent, gaseous effluent from the Devil's asshole swimming down his lungs. He tried to move, but some intangible force held him at bay. He was able to swing the light and follow the beam as it cut through the density.

It showed him shapes.

Stunted, humanlike forms lurking closer. They had the build of elves, of gnomes, tall as dwarfs. They were funny-boned with lopsided heads. Eyes flicked open on six, seven, twelve of them, and each was a yellow scab of neon. Greg screamed and felt his bowels surrender, filling the seat of his pants to a bulge the size of a soft-ball before going flat and running down his legs like pancake batter.

After he chucked out the last few squirts, the mist faded. Blew away as if it and its curious occupants had never been. There was no trace. No smell in the air, no farts ripping the night.

Just the feel of shit in his pants.

FIFTEEN

Greg had a night. And what a night. A nightmare was more like it. He got himself washed up and changed, but he would never feel fully unsullied or purged. Last night was another warning—or was it a sinister game? Just a little fun for the demon. He didn't know. He got on his channel after getting cleaned up and told his audience what he had learned. Some believed him, others didn't. That's the way it always was. He couldn't capture everything LIVE or on his cameras, especially since the cameras were spurting out like dying batteries. Sometimes these *things* knew he was filming or hoping to catch a piece of something verifiable. And when he'd let his guard down, they'd show themselves.

That was like anything in life, though.

You took your eyes off the road for one moment, and an animal went skipping across your hood. There were many such examples.

With the sun up, helping to dispel the night and its denizens back to the shadow realms, Greg was ready for a little side trip from the house. There was very little information on this house on the Web, and left with nothing—no help from the authorities who were paying him—he would seek out help from the locals. *If* they were willing to work with him. He wasn't so sure. His last foray into the town of Amityville made him feel unwelcome.

Breaking out his phone, he gave a quick update on his channel. Typing in that he was heading into town for some information-gathering purposes and to find something new to eat since the sandwich shop's employees were weird and strange. He hoped to gather some vital bits to help him in his purging of this toilet demon from Hell.

Closing the door behind him, Greg took in a whiff of the morning air. He smelled the salt breeze of the sea, fresh pine, and woodsmoke trailing out of chimneys. Before he began the day, he walked to the backyard and stared.

The grass was green, strewn with some pine cones and needles. Nothing abnormal and no smells of anal ruptures. Just pure heaven of spruce and sea breeze.

"Maybe I'm just hallucinating these things. Maybe it's a gas leak?"

What he knew for sure was, the shit that evacuated his bowels and splashed his legs was very real.

Very real indeed.

———

Frank Plunger and his family were cutting across the state for a warmer climate when little Justin, his ten-year-old boy, tugged on the headrest of his seat and told his daddy how awfully bad he had to take a whiz.

Frank was guiding his Volvo station wagon out of the thick pine forest that stood tall above Amityville, split with a snaking two-lane blacktop that terminated fifty miles north at his hometown. Frustration at why Justin decided not to tap his father's shoulder during the wooded drive, back where eyes wouldn't interfere with one answering the call of nature, was present in Frank's voice.

"Son, we were just in the woods! You could have gone then."

"Frank, honey, there's no need to yell at him. He didn't have to go then." Alison turned to her son and cooed, "Did you, sweetie?"

"No," he told her with the innocence of a ten-year-old with big fucking bowl-shaped hair sprouting from his head like a mound of brown weeds. His eyes were brown, too, round as chocolate coins, they were. His knees were buckling as he held his crotch.

"Frank, he has to go, find somewhere to pull over!"

"Would you look around?" he told her, waving his hand across the dashboard. "If he hops out here, everyone will see his penis! Then what? We'll be known as that one family who gave permission for their boy to go outside and empty his bladder all over their town!"

"You're being ridiculous," Alison said with a cutting glare. "Nobody is going to care if a little boy goes pee!"

"Yeah, well, I'll do what I think is right, if that's okay with you!"

Justin's bladder was primed to rupture the more his parents fought. Couldn't his dad see that he really needed to go? He would be one minute! One fucking minute to piss, zip, and be back in the car. It wasn't a big deal. But then again, his dad was always making a big deal out of everything.

"Look, there's a house down this street." Frank gestured, leaning forward to see it poised above the road, rising off an incline.

Alison looked around, out each car window. "Frank, the area is vacant. This is the only house here. Justin, just go outside and pee."

"Defying me, woman?"

"No. I just—"

"Justin," his dad said, turning angrily in his seat, his face as red as a beet from the seatbelt choking his neck. "You are not an animal! When you're in town, you will be civilized, and you will go up to that house like a gentleman and ask politely to use their bathroom."

"Frank, are you insane?" Alison asked, shaking her head at his suggestion. "He's not going to go up to someone's house and ask to use the potty."

"I told you to stop using that childish word. It's *bathroom*! He's going to use the *bathroom*, not the potty!"

"I'm going with him," Alison insisted, leaving the car and helping her son out of his seat. "I'm assuming you'll wait for us," she said to her husband, staring down at him from outside, a light mist of fog rearing skyward behind her.

"Of course, just hurry up."

"Come on, Justin."

They went up the steps and Alison knocked on the front door. "Hello? I'm sorry to bother you." She waited, then knocked again.

"I don't like this house, Mom."

"Why?"

Should he tell her, given the state she was in? She might have been on his side, but boy, get her riled, and she could be as mean as a rattlesnake in a bag on fire. Right then, her face was something akin to a skinned cherry, and her voice was fast and to the point, a bit of steam with each word.

"I don't know. Nothing, never mind."

She knocked again, louder this time. "Hello?"

Justin wasn't sure what it was about the house that rubbed him the wrong way, but it was bad. Even the floorboards of the porch were suspect. He swore he could hear a skittering, shifting motion beneath. "Mom?"

"What is it? I'm trying to get the owners to the door

71

so we can use the . . . *bathroom*," she said, her venomous tone spraying from her mouth. "HELLO!"

"I don't have to go anymore, Mom."

"Oh, don't start with that. I know you do. Screw it, you'll just go around the side of the house. If they catch you, I'll clean it up. Okay?"

"Okay, Mom."

She was turning them both around when the door opened.

"Hello?" Alison called, her demeanor never faltering. "Hello? Is anyone going to say anything?"

"What's going on over there?" Frank shouted from the car, agitated as usual.

"Nothing! We're almost done. Hold on!"

Justin swallowed as his mom practically dragged him into the house. "Hello . . ." She looked around. "Is anyone here?" Her voice dropped a degree lower. "The place looks abandoned."

Yeah, Justin was thinking, *or haunted*. That's what it was, a haunted house. Not that he'd ever seen one, apart from television. "Where's the bathroom?"

"This way," Alison said, as if she were privy to the blueprints.

The first door was down a hallway. She swung it open. "There, see?"

Justin did and felt somewhat relieved, but not fully. It might have been clean and sparking, but that's what made his nerves hold tight. Why was this toilet so clean and everything else they had seen was in need of repairs and deep scrubbing?

"Justin, please hurry. I don't want your dad to come up here and have one of his fits."

"I will."

She shut the door and waited.

Justin fronted the toilet and worked himself free. He started pissing, forcing it to hurry up by clenching his abs. The pressure worked and he was almost finished when a great suctioning sound arose from the bowl, plugging his ears with a wail that pierced his brain like acid. His hands flew up to his ears as he was forced forward until a faint *pop* inside his belly could be heard. He tried to scream for help but his voice wasn't working. It had been taken from him by the suctioning bowl. His stomach split open at the waist, drawing wide as ribbons of intestines went into the bowl like they were tumbling down an invisible slide, dragging everything out of him. An expulsion of blood blew from his mouth with such intense force that it took the lower jaw, ripping it off his face and sucking it down with everything else. A final heave of pressure folded him backward, lifting him off his feet with a gravitational pull that yanked his corpse into the toilet.

Alison came in after hearing something weird, and what she saw opened her mouth as wide as a coffee can and she screamed, "JUSTIN!" Blood and meat and bones were bubbling in the bowl water, roiling just like the child broth in a cauldron. The skull broke the surface and Alison saw her son's eyes, as clear as she remembered them. Both waxed over, then ran from the sockets like two taps gushing gravy.

She let her lungs blow with a final scream, then fainted.

And it was a bad place to faint because a ghostly fog slithered from the toilet tank and took her by the hair, dragging her toward it.

———

"Okay, Alison, I've had about enough!" Frank was in the house now, happy nobody was here because that meant he could do those things to his wife he only did behind closed doors. She acted like she didn't like it, but she did. At least, he thought so. "Alison, you're going to get it now! Where the hell are you two?"

He heard the toilet flush to his left and marched over there, his eyes inflamed and red. He slammed the door open, ready to unleash the mother of all fucking tirades, but lost his speech when he saw Alison— naked, dangling from some unseen thing on the ceiling. She was twisting around slowly like a side of beef in an icehouse. Above the tuft of blond hair between her legs, her skin was bloating. Everything, in fact, was starting to bloat now. Legs, arms, hips, feet, breasts, belly, neck, head—each part was filling out. Not with air, no, but with water . . . or some kind of liquid. He could hear the limbs expanding like water balloons held under a surging spigot. He was backing away, unable to form even a scream, completely under siege by an emotional rape.

"Ali— Alison—"

Then she exploded.

Like a bomb of water and blood, showering him with meat and bone flecks. He was pasted to the wall like a mural, splattered and dripping with his wife's anatomy. Strands of her stuck to his face and sat in his mouth. He took one look at the aftermath through eye-lids gummed with blood, and he ran.

He made it to the front door and was about to pull it open when a cackle from behind him went down his spine like a drop of ice-cold water. He started to shiver, turned, and saw—

A toilet monster. By God, he couldn't tell you other-wise because right there— believe it or ascribe it to fic-tion and tall tales—was a toilet monster. Imagine a big, scaly creature with huge trunk-like legs and arms ending in claws meant to shred the doors of bank vaults, stuffed into a one-size-too-small toilet costume. Its mouth, the tank, was crammed with hundreds of deadly teeth sharpened to spear points six inches long. It had eyes like bleeding knife wounds, and they were locked onto his, seeing past his tears and into a brain rotting with terror. He pissed and shit himself right there, prostrating to the demon. It ripped out a primal roar and swallowed him whole, not even chewing, just dropped its mouth over him like a whore deep-throating a cock, taking him all the way down.

SIXTEEN

Deputy Jake Urinal felt like a commando stalking his target in the tangle of a city street. Only this wasn't some highbrow metropolis of gleaming high-rises thrusting upward out of a concrete sea clogged with one-way streets and congested traffic, both motor and foot. This was Amityville. Quiet, isolated, humble, quaint Amityville.

Even so, there was a lot of excitement in keeping pace with The Ghost Hunter. Urinal felt like he was in his element, sticking to the shade of doorways and slinking up and shielding himself behind lampposts, using any and all available markers up and down the street as barriers to Greg's sight.

Balls put him on this mission under the pressure of Mayor Dump.

The chief said to him in that chiefly voice, "Deputy, don't screw this up. We need to keep tabs on that man. I just don't trust him for some reason."

When Urinal dared throw in an objection, Balls rose over him like a conquering flag raised over a defeated populace. "Don't question me, Urinal, just do as I command."

And that ended that.

Rule number one: never fuck with the chief.

Rule number two: do not—repeat—do not question his reasons.

Still, Urinal was a tad confused. *I don't see why I need to follow him. He's here to help us, to purge this horror from Amityville!*

That's what he wanted to say to the chief but instantly swallowed it down into the pit of his belly where, after he left the station, it climbed back up and sat in his mind. It really didn't make any sense, but rules were rules, and Urinal followed them to a *T*.

That's why he was a senior deputy with the Amityville Police Department.

Following Greg as he hopped across the street, Urinal waited for the man to duck inside a store and then made his move. He almost got hit as he entered the road blindly.

"Hey, what the hell, Deputy?" a passerby yelled, leaning on the horn.

Urinal waved, embarrassed by his blunder. He sidled up to the front of a flower store, shaking his head, feeling eyes up and down the street burning into him. He kept peeking out to see if Greg was leaving the store yet.

"Looking for me?"

Urinal stiffened like a popsicle in a freezer. He turned and saw Greg smiling at him. "Ghost Man, yeah, I was . . . No, I was just out on a foot patrol."

"You always follow visitors when on these patrols? Or is this just a special occasion?"

Urinal felt a knot in his throat.

"It's obvious you're following me, Deputy. I'm just trying to figure out why. Did I do something wrong? Break any laws?"

"Not at all, it's just,"—Urinal let his mind wander as

he scratched the back of his neck—"the chief asked me to keep tabs on you. That's all."

"Is there a reason?"

"Not that I know of." Urinal sighed, probably happy to relieve the absurdity of his position. "He's just . . . I dunno the right word."

"Nuts?"

Urinal offered no smile, just stared ahead. "I wouldn't say that. He's a great officer and man. Definitely not nuts. All of us Amityville residents owe a lot to him."

"I imagine."

"No, you don't."

Greg felt there was more here hiding behind the deputy's eyes. "Why don't you tell me, then? I'd like to know."

"About what?"

"Urinal, I'm talking about the Amityville House. Is there anything you can tell me? Anything at all that might help me understand what is in there? And why it prefers to haunt the shitters of this town?"

"Not *all* of them, not anymore. Just the Amityville House now."

"Okay, then enlighten me. Give me some history, if you will."

"History?"

"Of the toilet hauntings, the killings, any insight, please."

Urinal took him down a narrow alley made for deliveries and told him about the Toilet Raid that shook the town down for toilets. Greg couldn't believe it and wished he had recorded the conversation, but he feared moving. Urinal looked as unstable as a barrel of TNT hanging over a burn pit.

"You can't tell me anything else?"

"What more is there to tell? That's been on my conscience for a long time now. I won't ever get over my mistake."

"You still haven't told me what that was."

So Urinal laid bare his story. Supposedly, during a strike in one home, he was the first man in the stack of shooters going up the stairs. He swung into the bathroom and got so freaked out by what he saw that he hooked the trigger on the shotgun. The old lady on the toilet voiding dinner took the brunt of the buckshot. It turned her inside out and smacked her against the wall, exploding her body like a bag of raspberry jelly.

"I feel so bad, Greg. I should have controlled myself."

Greg didn't bother putting a hand on the man's shoulder. He figured if he showed sympathy, the deputy might take that as weakness, and he couldn't have that. No, he had to be strong.

And even with the nightmares of the old lady screaming at him as he busted down the door like King Kong and popped her with the shotgun haunting him nightly, Urinal had to regain control.

Instead of offering his touch, Greg said, "Listen, it was a mistake. According to you, a lot of mistakes like this were made. But it's over, okay?"

"Over?" Urinal laughed like a man in a straitjacket. "Nothing is over. Remember the body they found in the very house you're in? There's something evil here in Amityville. And you'd better hurry up and do something about it. Because if you don't, I'm afraid it'll do something to you."

"What does that mean? What are you talking about?"

"Just get rid of it."

Then Urinal was off, wiping away his tears.

SEVENTEEN

Going into town was a bust. Greg learned a bit, but it was nothing relatable to the case at hand. Other than what Urinal belched out, there was nothing surrendered by the citizens of the town. Not a nugget of information. Left holding his dick in his hands, Greg walked back to the house. He scratched his head at the Volvo parked alongside the curb just past the property line. It wasn't there when he left. He gave it a once-over from the porch and shrugged his shoulders.

"Probably someone ran out of gas."

He opened the door to the house and stopped at the sill. Again, expecting the worst scenario to come winging down the stairs for him, growling and starving, teeth resembling sharpened bowling pins and eyes as big and round as medicine balls, pink and dripping like placentas. What he got instead was a house that was silent and smelled like . . . ammonia. Nothing else.

But . . . was there a faint scent of . . . blood mingled with the chemical fumes?

He followed his nose to where it resonated strongest: the bathroom beside the kitchen.

He felt the heat of a thousand suns warm his face as he opened the door and saw—

A clean toilet.

Not a smudge or drop of blood anywhere.

"I could have sworn I . . . Whatever. If there's nothing here, then it's just in my mind."

He pulled his phone out as he walked back to his headquarters in the living room. He hit the **<LIVE>** button. "Okay, it's Greg, The Ghost Hunter here to drop you all a few interesting developments. Well, I say interesting because they are, but nothing to help me with what I'm dealing with."

As the visitors to the stream piled in, awaiting their master Ghost Hunter, he retold the tale related to him by Urinal, keeping his name out of it. He knew Balls and Dump were probably watching him right now, and if Urinal had the gonads to rip his heart out with his story, then he'd show him respect by expunging his involvement. He simply told his viewers that it was some random person on the street.

"Pretty crazy if you ask me," he said, finishing up the story. "I'm not sure if I believe it, though. I posed the story around to a few others in town, and most either ignored me or laughed and said I was ridiculous."

That much was true. After Urinal ran away, he tried his hand at asking several residents about the Toilet Raid, but nobody took him up on it. They acted as if any involvement with him was treason. So eyes were shut and lips were sealed. See no evil, speak no evil.

"I'm not sure, RaptornatorBGB, but maybe we'll uncover the extent of the raid yet. Could make a good side story to my blog. Okay, I've answered enough questions for now. I'm going to eat this grilled chicken wrap I picked up earlier and do some more investigative work. I hope to have something to report to you, and with any luck, I might get some actual verifiable content this time! And then all you naysayers will stop flapping your jaws. Until then, stay spooky!"

Clicked off, he put his phone on the charger.

Tearing the foil wrapper down, he started eating.

———

Three bites in, and a noise rattled him out of his comfort zone. He was standing now, staring at the ceiling.

The bathroom. There's something in the upstairs bathroom.

God, he hoped it was someone and not some*thing*.

Grabbing his phone, he hit the **<LIVE>** button, then whispered a few things. "Okay, just a quick note before I start filming, I'm setting my chicken wrap down because I'm hearing something above me. Listen . . ." He focused the lens on the ceiling as if that could pick up sound. "You hear that?" There were some shocked emote faces and laughing smiles mixing it up with the torrent streaming upward. "I'm hearing . . . I think I hear someone *shitting*."

More laughter faces erupted but there were encouraging comments too.

He started up the stairs, picking at some chicken lodged in his teeth. "Okay, I'm on the second floor now. The bathroom is down there, as you remember. Let's see what we have here. I'm not backing down, I'm rushing in this time." He turned the camera to himself. "You ready?" he asked his viewers, but mostly to pump himself up. He took the knob in his hand and pushed the door inward.

He almost jumped back into the hall, but he held his ground. Shaking as he saw the ghost of a man. Sebastian again, sitting there on the toilet in some pale blue shimmer, his pajama bottoms down at his ankles, his face a red mask of straining, his throat bulging with veins.

"Come on, come out of there," Sebastian said, just as

a *thunk* hit the water. "Ah, that felt good, burns too." He strained some more and another *thunk*, then three in a row slammed into the water. "Oh, some more is on the way!" He was stamping his feet on the ground, farts ripping out of him, long tearing flutelike squeals piping. "Okay, okay— Ah, much better."

"Are you all seeing this?" Greg whispered to the viewers. According to the feed, yes. Yes, they were all witness to this unreal event. Some were saying they had to refresh to ensure their connections were okay. The nonbelievers were believing. You *had* to believe after seeing this.

"Hey, quiet down!" Sebastian's ghost snapped, his eyes on Greg. "I'm trying to shit here."

Greg wanted to scream but kept his opinions to himself.

"Hey," Sebastian said, his face peering past his dick and into the toilet. "Hey, something's happening here."

Greg watched it unfold like a scene from a movie.

"Hey, what the— Help! Victoria! Help, something in the toilet's got me!"

Just then, a coldness seized Greg quickly departed him as a female clad in a robe walked right through him like he didn't exist. It had to be Sebastian's wife.

"Oh my God, Sebastian!"

"It's got me, baby!" he screamed.

But *what* had him was unknown. Until Greg and his audience watched in enraptured silence as the toilet stretched up to the ceiling like a sock pulled up a calf, completely enveloping Sebastian. Victoria screamed her throat raw as the engorged stem of the toilet turned rubbery and constricted down to the size of a toilet paper tube, the outline of her husband seen pressed against it, vacuumed tight, his limbs contorting then cracking, sounding like a bag of pretzel sticks being stomped on. As fast as the toilet took him, it shrank back to normal, then flushed. No blood, nothing.

Victoria made a run for it, and Greg went after her, still filming.

He wasn't saying a word, just keeping up with the ghost. She made it halfway down the staircase before the steps cracked open, and a mouth of ragged, splintery wood teeth took her down to the waist, chopping her in half. The lower part of her body tumbled down the remaining steps, dumping out copious reams of blood and viscera tangles. She landed with a squish at the bottom, then slid off on a pool of overspreading blood, riding its river down the hall where the ground floor bathroom door opened, admitting her through.

Greg was right there—right fucking there when the toilet transformed into a sharp tongue of pink slime, rolled her up, and chugged her into the bowl. There was a blinding crack of blue electricity and a cloud of blood, then a gentle flush.

And all was normal again.

Greg dropped his phone—good thing he had an OtterBox attached—then dropped to his knees, hands on his face. "I got it on film. I got it all on film. Wait . . . what?"

People were complaining of a black screen. Of having a visual of Sebastian on the toilet, then everything went scratchy before blanking out entirely.

"No! I filmed it all!"

He remembered how his surveillance cameras faltered and burnt out too.

This place didn't want to be filmed.

And for some reason, it liked toying with The Ghost Hunter.

EIGHTEEN

Was that real? Did he really just witness something so absurd yet so frightening it cored his reason out the window? Yes, it had to have been true, didn't it? Several hundred viewers of his channel could testify to that fact. So why was there conflict in his head over it? Because the reality was too much for the mind to handle. There was only so much room in the noggin for the paranormal—only so much space for things unseen and whispered to fit alongside the paradigm of logic.

Yet the truth was there; it varnished the house in blood and stuffed the air with the odor of fresh death. He saw it firsthand, and so did Chief Balls and the others who came into the house to clean it up.

A toilet demon. Not a ghost by any means, not a common poltergeist, but an influence from Hell, a spawn sourced to the world by the Father of Lies himself. The reasons for it being there were no more relevant than why it did what it did. It just *was*, and he wasn't sure he could turn it away. Wasn't sure if he was strong enough because he didn't wield the proper power or scepter to send that demon kicking and screaming back to the void.

Subscribers were cheering him on during his absence, telling him in a determined fashion that he was more than capable of dealing with this subversive horror. And to not let doubt dictate his course of action. They could glorify him with praise and pomp, and still, he felt inadequate for the task. The weight of it crushed him and drained whatever weapon he had left in a rusty arsenal. He was striving to pull himself out of the deep end, but it was like kicking up from the bottom of a river surging with rapids while chained to cinder blocks.

What am I going to do? he mused to himself. *I've never dealt with something so wicked in my life. This is beyond my means. I might have to recommend a more powerful body. A sorcerer, maybe, if there ever was one.*

Feeling unplugged, worn down, and wrung empty, he picked up his phone and took a walk outside.

He stared at the screen, at the digits spilled across the top. Mayor Dump's number. Should he call it? Tell him what he really thought about this place? About his impotence in extinguishing this malefic heartbeat in the house?

He hit the **<CALL>** button.

This was it. The moment when it all came crashing down.

———

Mayor Dump was in one of his moods. Yes sir, he was a mite angry with the world and the town and Greg, The Ghost Hunter, in particular. He wasn't sure if he liked that man. No, he was certain he hated him. Ever since he poked fun at his name on the LIVE feed, it irked him that this fella was in town—the very same man they were relying on to exterminate this threat before a bustling tourist season. He was in his office as usual, on his eighth cup of strong black with extra sugar, sweating, his tie loosened, his blazer a victim of coffee stains. His white hair, normally combed slick off the brow, was disheveled, his eyes bloodshot.

Time was ticking, and he was not in the mood for any excuses. He hoped Greg was almost finished with the task. Waiting on word was like walking a tight rope of razors over a punji pit full of sewage runoff and piranhas.

The phone rang and right away, his hand leaped to it, tore it from the cradle, and brought it to his ear. "Greg, is that you? You better have some good news, I—"

"Sir, this is Melissa. I was just wondering if you wanted any lunch. They're ordering now."

"Lunch?" Mayor Dump pulled away from the phone and looked at it like he was holding a piece of shit—someone else's shit. "Lunch?" he said again, this time with some spit and piss in his words. "If I wanted lunch, Melissa, I would have screamed to you through the fucking door! I told you to never, ever, ever call me for lunch! You know I can hear you through the door! You never call me on here, you always come to the door! Why is this any different today, huh?"

Melissa was shaking like she was naked, buffeted by cold winds and ice water. "I— I'm sorry, sir. I didn't mean to make you upset."

"UPSET? DO I SOUND UPSET?"

"Yeah."

"I'M FURIOUS! YOU HEAR? I'M FURIOUS! YOU'RE FIRED! GET THE HELL OUT OF THIS BUILDING!"

He slammed the phone down and caught his breath. Red-faced, his fists balled up, he beat on his desk and stomped his feet.

The phone rang again.

He let out a maniacal chuckle as he grabbed it and

87

brought it slowly to his ear. "Melissa," he said, dragging her name out long and sharp, "if you think apologizing to me is going to reverse my decision, you have — Oh, Mr. Ghost Hunter, Greg." Dump dialed his temper down a few levels. "I've been waiting for your call. No, Melissa is my—was—my assistant. Tell me some good news. I need it more than ever."

Greg had thought long and hard about what he would say, even going over it several times to shake out the kinks, and hoped he wouldn't stumble in his delivery. He sucked in a breath and let it out. "I'm not sure I'm the one who can rid this house of its demon."

Mayor Dump was silent for a full minute. Greg could hear him breathing, could even feel the air thicken as if he were about to snap out, then calmed himself.

"Greg, I've been having a morning. Everything has gone wrong. Everything that should be going right has flipped over and shown me the bad side of the rotten log, if you catch my drift. I need to hear something better than what you're telling me, so I'm giving you one more chance to rethink your decision."

There was no rethinking on his part; Greg was firm. Vanquishing this horror was not in his wheelhouse. He was not the force required to exorcise this invader. They needed someone stronger—likely a special priest—not Greg, The Ghost Hunter. He dealt with lesser poltergeists and spirits, not demons. Demons were for the church to handle. Greg explained this to Dump, and still, the man refused to believe the facts. He exploded with rage, his face purpling as he spoke.

"What do you mean? You're telling me you can't kill this toilet? What? You're not going anywhere, do you hear me? ANYWHERE!"

"I think it's best if I leave town and send someone else in my stead. Someone qualified to help you."

"*You're* not leaving town," Dump said with all the threat of a knife at Greg's neck. "Try it, smart guy, and I'll have Balls throw up barricades and smoke you out. You're not leaving here. You have a job to do! I'm paying you! Good money! You're not leaving my town without first killing that toilet."

"I understand your anger, Mayor. I do. But you have to put yourself in my shoes and see this through my eyes. I'm a ghost hunter. Not a demon destroyer! I don't work with demons—never have! How can you expect me to do this?"

"So that's it? You're just quitting? You think it's that simple, do you? Just unplug and walk away?" Dump laughed with the grating of stone on sandpaper. "Listen here, buddy. I don't like you and you don't like me. That's fine. But what isn't fine, is you telling me you're going to leave! Well I have some news for you, smart guy. If you try and leave . . . you're finished."

"And what's that supposed to mean?"

Greg could nearly see the man's evil lips slashing open with a grin that would spook a rattlesnake. "Use your imagination."

Greg felt a tightening in his chest. He remembered what Urinal had told him. About the raid and the citizens who died during that operation. If anyone had the clout to order a man's death, it was Mayor Dump. And as unstable as he sounded through the phone, Greg had no doubt in his mind that the guy was a hair's breadth away from popping off an order that would see Greg's head riding a spear on his lawn.

"Okay . . . I'll try."

"Try? Let me tell you something. Nobody *tries*—you either do it or you don't. There is no maybe, no possibly, no try. Just *do*. So you go back in that house and deal with this or be dealt with. Your choice. Choose wisely."

89

Greg's mind was crammed with a vision of Mayor Dump sliding shells into the breach of a shotgun as he spoke. "I'll do it."

The smile on the mayor's face was that of a genuine politician: perfect white teeth in a poster board grin and empty eyes. "That's what I wanted to hear, Greg. Now tourist season will flourish on time." He paused as if in thought about the money flying into town. "I'm cutting your stay time down to one day. Get it done."

The phone cut off, and Greg checked his. "He hung up. He's dead serious." A million questions entered Greg's head, all of them screaming for answers. "I guess I have no choice."

Nineteen

This was it. This was the time of reckoning. He brought his phone up, fixed his hair, and checked his teeth. He hit the **<LIVE>** button. "Folks, good to see you," he said, dropping his usual introduction. His face was drawn tight and his eyes were huge and glassy. "So I just had an interesting conversation with the mayor, and I've decided I'm going to see this job through. No matter the difficulties that lie ahead, I will do my utmost to bring peace to this house and this town. I'm an empath and paranormal investigator, and I will execute my job to the best of my abilities. And if, for some reason, I fail, then you will all be witnesses to my demise. From here on out, I will be LIVE. Let's just hope it sticks this time." He took several deep breaths. The house was there in front of him, a tower of death and blight. It seemed to look down on Greg, smirking at his plan. "I'm doing this for my followers. I have one hundred ninety-nine followers, and I'm fishing for that one extra. If you're watching this and you haven't subscribed, please do so now! I can really use the help here." He waited, watching his feed, answering questions while dreading what lay ahead. The subscriber notification dinged and his eyes widened. "It looks like I just hit two hundred subs. Thank you, FecalTerminator1994! So here we go."

TWENTY

"Before I set foot in this house, I have to tell you now that everything you see will be real. To all the naysayers out there, and the ones trying to call my bluff, keep that out of my chat or you'll be blocked. There is nothing cinematic here—no props, no effects, nothing. Just me and my phone and this house. Oh, and the two most coveted items in my ghost-fighting kit: a crystal and a crow feather. They have kept me safe during my travels, and I can only assume these two charms have served as the shield protecting my life in this house since day one. Instead of having them out of reach, both will be wielded by me. This is the endgame here, folks. No more playing. It's time to earn some money. Also, I apologize in advance for my lack of interaction. I won't be responding to questions until the end of the stream —if I'm still among the living. I've said my peace. Please, if you're a believer, send me any blessings!"

Affixing his camera to a bracket and then to his coat, he entered the house.

The feeling was one of unauthorized access. He was a violator of a tomb, a trespasser on holy land—in this case, *un*holy land. His footfalls were echoes captured and deflected from outer voids. A heavy, unnerving cold sat in the air. It caused his teeth to chatter and frost to plume from his breath. With crystal and feather firmly held, he cut to the left, past the dining room and kitchen, and faced the bathroom door.

"I can do this."

He opened it and thrust both feather and crystal ahead of him like a sword cleaving aside a quilt of spiderwebs. "You," he said, directing his voice toward the toilet. "Leave this place at once! I order you to uproot your evil and relocate back to whatever dimension conveyed your presence!" For a moment, he felt like a fool, shouting at a toilet. He wanted to laugh. He wanted to shrug, call an Uber, and peace out of Amityville for good. "What do you got, huh? Illusions?! You're weak, you're a pathetic demon! A shit demon! A shit demon from shit Hell! You're nothing! Vacate this house at once! Leave this town alone!" A rumbling seized the house. Shaking it with violent percussions, causing studs to rip through drywall and beams to shake away ceiling plaster. The floor shuddered, fracturing the floorboards throughout the house, upstairs and down, like the sun-cracked pattern of a dry lake bed. Greg staggered, the imbalance of the floor pushing him around. He grunted, catching himself with his elbow on the wall. An incandescent rupture of light pulled his awareness back into the bathroom. The toilet was ringed by a circle of fire climbing higher to the ceiling. The floor, too, spurting with jets of flame coming together, exploding with a fireball that went right over him and licked the wall black. He was on the ground, sobbing and choking, rolling off to the side just in time to avoid another rush of flame that singed the back of his pants and coat with ash.

Immediately on his feet, gasping out of the hallway, he was now in the foyer. "I can't do this! It's too strong! I can't! Dump, Balls, Urinal, if you're there, I can't do it!

Help!" Overhead, the ceiling was bubbling like hot cheese on a pizza, going brown then black, striating with a network of intersecting dark ribbons spreading out like tree roots. Superheated, the veins bulged, fluttered open with spurts of steam, and spilled liquid flame around him like raindrops. He cried out as a blue ball of fire the size of a gumdrop hit the meaty portion of his hand and went right through it, taking out a wad of flesh and blood to plop and sizzle on the ground. In pain, he almost dropped the crystal but refrained from doing something so stupid. He had to believe these totems were still defending against his death.

Torn with agony in his hand, he screamed, "I'm out of here! Fuck this!"

He tried the door and it opened. Relieved, he ran out—

Right back into the house. He turned and found himself in the master bedroom. "What is going on? Help!" Realizing he was letting his fear of the house control him, he managed to shrink his dread down a notch and take control of the situation as best he could. "It seems like this demon is forbidding my exit. I have to do something, only I'm at a loss." A knocking on the door silenced his voice. He looked, expecting it to fly open or fall to the floor like a dune of sand. But the knob twisted and the door opened slowly, then slammed open, admitting a storm of *hornets*.

"Bees!"

Compulsion to preserve his life stripped his fear. He battled his way through the vicious horde. They struck from all directions, overwhelming his defense of slapping hands and petty kicks. He spit and cursed and swung the crystal in arcs with all the power of a swordsman slaying a stampede of the undead. He cut a wedge in their formation and struck out for the door, hewing and slicing thick curtains of hornets sent tumbling to the floor like grains falling from a riven sack. He made the door and hurled his bulk through it, turning immediately to face another rush—

But the room was empty. The dead hornets washed away like fog burning off at sunrise. "I'm losing it! Did anybody see that? Tell me I'm not the only one!" As he lifted the camera to see the results, a curious smoke swirled up from the floor not three feet away. It started low, rising to form a helix, lifting and widening to frame a human body.

A dead body. A corpse walker.

Greg cried out as the flaking, diseased ruin of flesh and meat with eye sockets pocketed with red blisters and teeth like cracked fence posts reached out for him with nails like the talons of a hunting hawk. Standing his ground, believing this to be another illusion weaponized against him by the demon, he shouted, "You are not real!" at the top of his lungs and drove the crystal forward, his body racing behind his outstretched arm like a cavalryman galloping toward an adversary. The crystal's apex slaughtered the apparition, storming through its body which blew away like smoke from a bellows.

"HA! I knew it! Come on, demon, you can do better than that!"

Full of himself now, hubris in his blood, puffing out his chest, he went down the stairs, frightful of the flames in the hallway but not enough to turn away. No, Greg was certain he could deal with the toilet the same way he had dealt with the other entities in his line of work. Until the air around him grew dark, as shadows pressed through walls and floor and swallowed him, breaking open with branching lines and apertures as blue as cobalt. "What is this? What is this?!" Suddenly, the shadows dissolved and tore apart as clouds of ravens. Hundreds and hundreds of tiny ravens the size of pet store mice flocked to attack him, diving toward him like German Stukas, pummeling him with beaks as sharp as chips of glass. Again, he waved his crystal, but unlike last time, there was no effect. "It's not working! It's not working!" The beaks pecked at his exposed flesh, drawing out beads of blood resembling perspiration.

Then he remembered the feather.

He lashed out at the ravens, circling the feather overhead and around him, disbursing the ravens that detonated in showers of black smoke like flak over a battlefield. Once the last of the ravens faded from sight, Greg, wild-eyed and shaken to his soul, felt his heart striving to burst. "I don't know how much more I can take. I know this is all unreal, purely distractions and terrors from the demon. But I don't know—"

As he was talking, his voice petered out when he heard the pipes in the walls straining with fatigue. First to his side, next under his feet in the kitchen, and then from both bathrooms, he heard the pipes whine with distension. Before he could properly fix his voice, the walls and floor and ceiling ripped open, exploding with water. Hundreds of gallons of toilet water rushing through the house, pouring down the steps in a raging torrent. The water was at his knees in seconds and climbed higher in just a few blinks of his eyes. The interior was inundated, flooded basement to ceiling—a goddamn fish tank full of toilet water.

Struggling with indecision and fretting about how long he could hold his breath before his lungs fried, he became aware of an impossible element here.

I can breathe, he thought. *I can breathe!*

But he couldn't talk, not without sounding garbled and funny.

He wondered why he was spared, then the question was answered in the form of a motherfucking shark. A great white, a hulking machine of teeth and orbits blown open with red balls of fire as bright as traffic lights. It gave one look at him and came forward, wagging its tail fin like a hungry dog. It swiftly tore past as Greg ducked, leaving a trail of vertical bubbles from his scream. He swam into the kitchen, hiding around the island. He peeked up and saw the shark. It was in the dining room, floating there like a ghost. Its eyes blazed as its mouth fell open to the width of a mountain cave and rushed over, causing turbulence in the water.

Greg screamed more bubbles and went low.

The shark blew by overhead, nearly taking him out with its propulsion. It hit the cabinets and went through them, disappearing.

The water too—gone, just like that.

Greg gave himself the once-over. He was wet and dripping and his clothes were soaked and he clung to the crystal and feather. "No, that couldn't have been real." He smelled the smoke of the fire tearing up the house, popping knots in the studs. "Shit!" He tried the front door again in one defiant move, but the knob burned the skin on his hand. He let go and screamed, watching as the brass fixture crumpled inward like hot plastic, dripping down the door in liquid gold streams, spotting the floor with sizzling burns.

In the confusion, the turmoil scraping his mind, he spun around, his crystal held tight, the feather frayed but intact. He choked on the air. At this rate, he'd spin to the floor and curl up and die inhaling the smoke. He wanted to cry but stopped himself. He remembered he was LIVE, and how awful would that look? He'd probably be turned into a GIF or a meme, something to bring joy to people.

Then he spotted it. Lying there under the coffee table.

"It can't be."

But it was. A goddamn Bible of all things. He couldn't believe his luck. The edges were worn as if from heavy use. He pocketed his feather and crystal and took it in his hands. When he held it up, there was a noticeable shift in the air around him, as if the tome were a weapon, purging a hole in the evil.

"Oh, you don't like that, do you?" he shouted. "So this is your kryptonite! Well, demon, it's high time to send your ass back to Hell!"

He was on his feet, a new energy driving him down the hall. He stopped and turned at the bathroom, and a burst of flame hurled him back, but he wasn't stopping. The demon's agitation at Greg acquiring the Bible told him this was the weapon to wield in the battle. He spoke to his subscribers, "This is it, hunters! I'll either survive or die, but this is it!"

Determined to end this menace, he entered the bathroom and was attacked immediately from all angles, first clouds of fire, then nests of screeching hornets, hundreds of ravens, crystal rainstorms, lightning cracking, sharks snapping at his feet, jets of fire shooting from the walls. It threw *everything* at him. The toilet lid flipped open and three babies were crushed in there— their faces fused into one ghastly whole, mouths ripping open with screams, eyes like purple jelly sparking with pink flames. Blood poured from the base of the toilet, sending out thick waves to overflow his feet and sluice around his ankles.

"YOU WILL LEAVE! I COMMAND THEE OUT OF HERE!"

Yeah, it felt good to say that. Like some priest expelling a demon out of a movie. He thought of that horror movie with the crucifix-masturbating little girl in it but couldn't come up with the title. Placing the Bible in front of him, he continued to shout commands and hurl curses to remove the malign tumor of the demon invader, "OUT! I CAST THEE OUT. IN THE NAME OF JESUS AND JOB AND ALL THOSE PEOPLE IN THE BIBLE! GET OUT! OUT! NOW!"

Maybe it was the last reserves of patience because out of the toilet bowl erupted a heavy, dense volume of prismatic-colored smoke, gushing like a foundry stack, thickening and coiling until forming a solid column. Greg was freaking out. He stepped back once then twice, just as the column angled with a sharp right and flew in his direction, spilling past him like a freight train off its rail. It stopped behind him.

He turned and saw—

A dinosaur. A velociraptor coming out of the smoke like a curtain was lifted for its emergence. Yes, the same sort of creature everyone gasped at in the theater during that scene in *Jurassic Park*. It rushed at him, screeching, the avian cords in its throat shrieking, its eyes narrowed, teeth like knitting needles.

In a move that surprised even himself, Greg spun and lifted the Bible. The raptor hit the target, dispersing like ash in high wind. The word of God saved him and reinstilled the faith he lost so long ago. Demon storms raged as he fought to defeat the evil. He was shaken, disturbed, heart rattling like a ball in a spray can. The ceiling was sucked away as a cloud as gray as brain matter took its place, emitting blue flashes that became whipping strokes of lightning. They struck around him, tearing through the walls and scorching the floor.

Then Greg had a moment of clarity. Everything seemed to slow down. At this time, he was mindful of his surroundings. The toilet . . . the lid was open and a storm of blood was bubbling inside.

"I KNOW WHAT TO DO!" he shouted over the incessant cracks of lightning. "YOU WILL FOREVER BE VANQUISHED!"

With this outburst and another shocking move that

sent his viewers closer to their phones, he tossed the Bible into the toilet. It hung in the air, a suspended book fluttering like a leaf caught in an updraft. He watched as it sailed and then found its mark, splashing down into the blood.

Greg leaped after it and reached a hand out, his finger hooking the flushing lever. "GO BACK TO SHIT HELL WHERE YOU BELONG!" The toilet flushed, and the demon spoke. It spoke, not as a toilet would sound, but as a beast, a monster—a cheated, defeated roar that left the toilet bowl and lashed its way through the house, echoing, growing to ear-piercing and intolerable decibels. It busted windows, bowed walls, ripped shingles off the roof, and caused the lawn—back and front and sides—to rise and split open. The house was tottering, shaking siding to the ground, causing nails to pop, doors to fly off hinges, beams to split. The kitchen exploded, the sink crushed like a beer can, piping twisted and pulled from the walls and floors and flung to bounce through the house.

Terrified, on the way to having a stroke, Greg backed away, keeping his eyes on the toilet as it turned bright red like a hot coal, then shimmered like a heat mirage, going pliant as warm clay, then peeling open in slabs, blood spilling. It crumbled layer by layer until finally, the toilet was a hot, steaming mound of offal and bones and pipes, a tower of a hundred skulls, its shell wilting like superheated plastic.

Greg let himself breathe as the storm and the madness retreated with the death of the toilet. He did it. He exorcised the demon. He smiled and laughed. And continued laughing.

TWENTY-ONE

It could have been a minute or ten, maybe twice that long. Greg laughed his throat raw, distorting his voice with a croak akin to a drill sergeant shouting at cherries in boot camp. Time had no meaning and reality had twisted its angles long enough for Greg to forget how he managed to walk away from the house with all of his gear and stand outside under a misty sky. Caught up in the excitement—the shock of dread—he neglected to inform the subscribers and viewers in the feed.

He fondled the phone on his chest, amazed it was still there after everything. He plucked it from the bracket and faced it toward him. No damage was evident, and this, too, amazed him. For the battle had been fought hard and dirty, it was a surprise there wasn't even a scratch on the screen. And, to make it more incredible, the LIVE feed was still active.

"As you can see," he started saying, his voice a harsh croak, "I'm still here. I made it. I can't believe it. Did everyone see what I went through?" He was pleased to see they had, and they responded in kind by popping hearts and hugging emotes, some kisses, the whole river of them floating up in a digital swarm.

"Thank you."

"Thank you."

"You too!"

"Thank you."

"That's very kind."

After replying to each comment, he brought up the Uber app and requested a ride. As he waited for it to arrive, he reflected.

The demon had perished, and Greg was the victor. But it was hard for him to believe. The entire affair was like walking the corridors of a fun house, a psychotropic labyrinth of smoke and mirrors and Hollywood effects. In previous cases, the most he'd ever encountered with any physical projection were shadows sweeping past windows or walls. Nothing compared to the evil of the Amityville House and its dark passenger, now a terrible memory. This battle renewed his faith in God and gave him an extra weapon —a fortified arsenal of power in his mind. No longer would he fear the extra-dimensional travelers. He would stand and face them. Siphon their energy.

The sound of an engine rolling up the road lifted his face away from the phone. It was the chief and his deputy. Greg waited for them to come over. He clipped the phone to the bracket, ensuring it was still LIVE.

"Ghostbuster," Urinal said, striding up with a rare smile on his face. "You did it! I watched you do it. It's gone?"

Greg nodded. "Flushed back to Hell."

"Thank you," Urinal said, a tear balling up in the corner of his eye. "I can finally seek peace with my sin. You have no idea the good you've done for this town. You're a hero, Greg."

A hero? Was this what it felt like to be a hero? Like a beaten and battered thing, a mind in conflict, a brain and body razed and left with patches of trauma? "I'm not a hero, Urinal. I was paid to do a job and I did it. It's over."

"That's what all heroes say," Urinal replied, never dropping his smile. Until Chief Balls walked up, the Winston hanging off his lip. "Chief, I was congratulating our hero—"

"I don't see no hero, just a Ghost Man."

Urinal pinned his lips closed, knowing it was best to keep quiet than to say anything that could send Balls into a whirlwind of anger.

"Chief Balls," Greg said, taking a long look at the attitude on his face and the cigarette. "Mind if I bum one of those from you? My pack"—he patted his jacket pocket and water seeped out—"is mush."

Balls reached into his pocket and tossed him the whole pack. "There's a couple more in there. You've earned them."

There were numerous questions Greg wanted to throw out to Balls, but what was the point? Would it do him any good to rile him up by starting an argument? The demon was gone, the house was empty, and the town could breathe. Yet, Chief Balls was there like he had something to say.

"Something on your mind, Chief?" Greg asked him, fishing a cigarette out. Balls snapped a lighter. "Thanks," Greg said, inhaling deep and letting the smoke course from his nostrils.

"My mind, you ask?"

Greg nodded.

"Nope."

Greg dragged a hit. "I wasn't gonna say anything, Balls, but letting this sit isn't doing me any good. So break it down for me, will you? What's your problem with me?"

"Problem?"

"Don't act like you don't have one with me. You've

been spitting citrus in my eyes since I met you. So what is it?"

Balls flicked ash off his Winston and removed his shades. "I don't like social media people. The truth of the matter is, folks like you are a stain on this world. You think you're so big and bright and important with that camera in your face. All of your little subscribers, as you call them, are just as ass-backward as you." He dropped the filter and stepped on it. "Social media is a curse, Ghost Man, and you're only adding to it."

That was the big problem? Chief Balls wasn't particularly fond of social media? Of all the things to raise his hackles about. Greg couldn't help but smile and choke on the smoke coming up his throat.

"Social media hate, huh?"

"That's right."

"Well that I can handle. It's okay, Balls, I have lots of hate but more love than you'll probably ever feel the rest of your life."

The chief glared as Urinal bit his lip, worrying what could happen if Balls lost it.

"I'm finished here. It's time for me to go."

Balls turned around and saw the Honda Accord pulling to the curb.

"Yep, that's my ride." He extended his hand to Urinal, who took it and pumped it hard. "Urinal, it's been real."

He locked eyes with Balls. "Chief . . . thanks for the smokes."

Then Greg was in the backseat of the Honda, his face forward, looking away from the house and the two officers.

He still had a phone call to make.

Surprisingly, Mayor Dump was exuberant. He couldn't be happier, even if his dick was getting sucked. He had one of those pre-elect smiles on his face, the same sort of smile given to cameras. "Greg, I'm happy about the outcome. I knew you could do it! Never doubt yourself! I suppose we don't have to worry about it ever coming back either?" He posed this as a question.

"Fingers crossed, Mayor. I took care of that thing the best way possible."

"Tell me how you did it, Greg."

Greg took him for a ride, detailing every occurrence and nightmare shoved against him in the house.

"Unbelievable! I mean, I saw some of it LIVE, but it's just hard to believe something like that happened."

"Believe it, Mayor Dump, it happened. As for now, I'm off to the airport and from there, home. By the way, when can I expect payment?"

"I signed it this morning. The check is in the mail."

"Awesome news. I guess I'll take my leave now."

"You have a safe flight, Greg, and . . . no hard feelings, okay?"

Greg had plenty he wanted to say, but as with Balls, he kept it bottled up. There was no reason to add fuel to a hot coal bed. Might as well just let it burn out. "No hard feelings."

———

Dump hung up the phone. "You piece of shit." He laughed. "He may have gotten rid of that toilet, but he's still a piece of shit! I'm done being nice." His stomach started bubbling. "Damn, I knew I shouldn't have had that extra burrito." He made his way to the bathroom. Working his belt loose, he dropped his pants and sat down, immediately dropping a waterslide of shit. He smiled. "Thank God I don't have to worry about doing this anymore."

Too busy laughing and shitting, he didn't have time to react or scream when the toilet bowl widened out to the size of a kiddie pool, then bared teeth a foot long that curled inward like a rattler's fangs. A tongue of pink slime thrust inside his anus with an impaling force, bursting from his mouth, the tip whipping out and coiling his neck. Locked in place, the mouth sprung shut, snapping around him like a bear trap, crushing him to a pulped smear of blood and tissues and bone chips. And with a flush, he was no more.

The demon cackled.

The following pages include various images from the film.

Used by Permission.

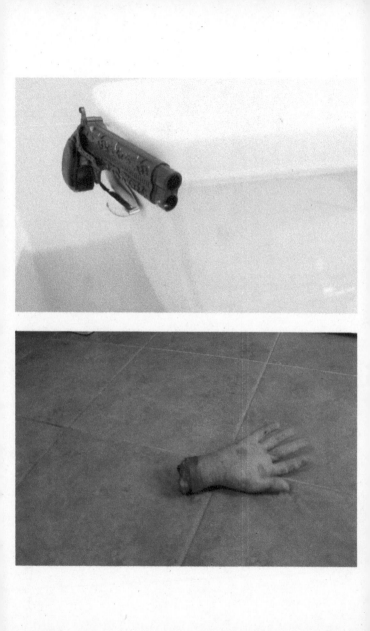

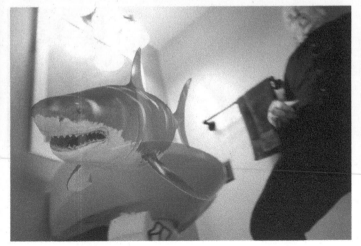

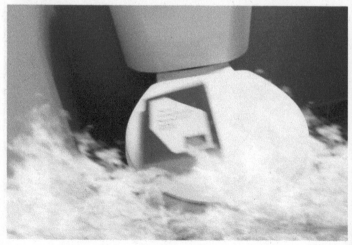

THE RETRO MASS MARKET COLLECTION

COLLECT THEM ALL!

- ☐ HELLRAISER: THE TOLL
- ☐ FRIGHT NIGHT
- ☐ RE-ANIMATOR
- ☐ HARDCORE
- ☐ WISHMASTER
- ☐ HELLRAISER: BLOODLINE
- ☐ TITAN FIND
- ☐ CREATURE
- ☐ VAMP
- ☐ SCARED TO DEATH
- ☐ OF UNKNOWN ORIGIN
- ☐ MANBORG
- ☐ ATTACK OF THE KILLER TOMATOES
- ☐ THE SPECIAL
- ☐ TAMARA
- ☐ FORBIDDEN ZONE
- ☐ COMMANDO NINJA
- ☐ LONG WEEKEND
- ☐ THE ODD JOB
- ☐ BLUE SUNSHINE
- ☐ THE BARN
- ☐ MOTORBOAT
- ☐ HOUSE SHARK
- ☐ HOUSE SQUATCH
- ☐ SHE KILLS
- ☑ AMITYVILLE DEATH TOILET
- ☐ SPLICE
- ☐ CUBE